NAUGHTY WISH

Brit Boys Sports Romance

J.H. CROIX

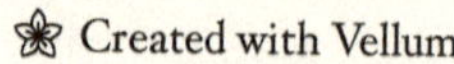 Created with Vellum

*For those who believe chance sometimes comes along by accident.
Never forget to look.*

***Sign up for my newsletter for information on new
releases & get a FREE copy of one of my books!***

http://jhcroixauthor.com/subscribe/

Follow me!
jhcroix@jhcroix.com
https://amazon.com/author/jhcroix
https://www.bookbub.com/authors/j-h-croix
https://www.facebook.com/jhcroix
https://www.instagram.com/jhcroix/

READER'S NOTE

When I wrote Out Of Bounds for this series, Jana was the side character who stole my heart. I *really* wanted to write her story even though her story hadn't been part of my plan for the series. Many readers asked me about her too, so I figured it was meant to be.

You might wonder why her sexy cop hero isn't a sports star. Oh well. He's not. I'm figuring by now you probably aren't reading my books for the sports. If you are, my sincere apologies. Jana's story belonged in this series, so that's where it is. It's hot, it's steamy, and it's fun. There's a dash of sports in it, but that's all. ;)

xoxo

JH Croix

NAUGHTY WISH

Jana

How to seduce a cop for Christmas
Flirt shamelessly when said sexy cop pulls you over.
Send naughty texts.
Sweet-talk him into dinner.
Melt... Panties, me, and more.
Wait a sec. This was supposed to be just a little harmless fun.
He's in *way* too deep.
So is my heart.

Finn

A fender bender lands Jana Sparks in my police cruiser.
All I'm supposed to do is give her a ride.
Instead, I'd like her to ride *me*.
She's bold, brash and beautiful.
I thought I was too cynical to fall for someone again.
Jana makes me so hot and so hard, I ache for her.

I can't keep my hands off of her, and I can't keep *her* from stealing *my* heart.
It was hers the first night we spent together.
I just have to make her believe it.

Chapter One

JANA

My car lurched forward with a loud crunch. I'd been about to take a sip of coffee, only to have it spill all over my blouse. "Dammit!" I muttered to no one. I'd been inching along in Seattle's morning rush hour traffic and just gotten thumped in the bumper by the car behind me. On top of wondering how bad off my bumper was, I had coffee all over me.

"Great, just great. Exactly how I want to start my day."

I had a habit of talking to myself, especially when I was annoyed. I was in the far right lane—thank God—and slowly inched over to the side of the busy freeway. Snagging a napkin, I wiped the coffee splashed on my hand and dabbed at my blouse. Just my luck to be wearing a white blouse today. Climbing out, I smoothed my skirt, my eyes catching on the lovely new coffee stain on the side. I watched as the car that had run into me nearly clipped another bumper as the man driving it pulled over onto the shoulder.

He climbed out, slamming the door behind him, and stalking over to me where I waited by the guardrail. "Don't even try to tell me this was my fault," he said with a glare.

He wore—I kid you not—a bright yellow, shiny tracksuit.

"How the hell is this my fault?" I asked, throwing a glare right back at him.

"You stopped too fast," he declared, smoothing his hand over his slick, dark hair and crossing his arms.

Oh fuck that. I was not taking the blame for this. "There's a rule. If you hit the person in front of you, you were too close. There's no way that was my fault," I countered.

Tracksuit rolled his eyes. He was so cocky, he took my annoyance to the next level.

"Fine. Let's call the cops," he retorted with a smirk.

"Fine, let's."

I whipped my phone out and tapped out 9-1-1. I quickly reported our fender bender and then slipped my phone back in my purse before crossing my arms and leaning against my car.

"We'll just wait."

Tracksuit rolled his eyes again and leaned against his car. A few minutes later, I could see the lights of a police car approaching through the traffic. The police vehicle pulled over behind our cars. Within seconds, the police officer was climbing out, at which point Tracksuit decided to announce again that I'd been going too slow.

"Officer, she was also looking down at her phone," he added.

My cheeks got hot, and I pushed my hips off of my car, spinning to glare at him. "I was *not* looking at my phone you asshole!"

It was at this opportune moment our friendly cop arrived beside us, glancing down at me. I looked up at him and my breath caught in my throat. Oh. My. Wow. I loved a man in uniform. All by itself, a uniform was hot. Throw in this police officer's dark brown hair, deep blue eyes and a face to make me melt, well, I kinda melted a little right there.

He had sculpted cheekbones, a strong nose, a square jaw, and a sexy shadow of stubble. And his mouth, oh my God, his mouth. He had full, lush lips and a dimple in his chin. Really, where the hell did he come from? They shouldn't make cops like him. It was dangerous. I would do anything he said right now. In fact, he could cuff me and take me away if he wanted.

I stayed quiet. I'd like to say I was strategically quiet, but I was actually speechless. That gave Tracksuit an opening.

"Not my fault. She was looking at her phone and slammed on her brakes," he announced.

Sexy cop eyed him for a moment and then looked to me. Oh this was just all kinds of bullshit. I got hot inside, probably a combination of the fact I was melting inside over sexy cop and angry with Tracksuit.

I glared at Tracksuit, temporarily forgetting about sexy cop. "I was *not* staring at my phone, and I did *not* slam on my brakes. I slowed down because I had to. In case you didn't notice..." I paused and gestured to the bumper to bumper traffic crawling along the crowded freeway "...it's rush hour."

I huffed and brushed my hair off my shoulder. Sexy cop glanced between us.

"Well this should be easy enough to resolve. You mind letting me check your phone?" he asked.

"Huh?" was my brilliant response.

"If I can confirm your phone wasn't in use, then it's easy."

There were laws about not using 'handheld devices' when driving, but I hadn't been using my phone so there was nothing to see. I handed it over without even thinking. Small problem though. As soon as I handed it to him, I realized he would see my screensaver, which was a picture of a penis. That's right. A penis. It was a joke. A friend had a bachelorette party and all the baked goods were naughty. My screensaver had a picture of a penis cake. It was so lifelike, I'd been unable to resist the urge to photograph it and proudly saved it to my phone. It made me laugh every time I looked at it. Great way to stay cheery.

I watched his eyes land on the screen and flick back to

me. My cheeks heated. His gorgeous mouth curled at the corner, just the tiniest bit, and I couldn't help but grin.

His gorgeous blue eyes glinted with mirth, but he didn't laugh. He finally spoke. "You need to unlock it for me."

I almost forgot to mention sexy cop had a British accent. Where in God's name did a British cop come from in Seattle? I didn't know, but he could talk to me all day. It was that awesome. I was downright flustered at this point, my body humming so hard I was almost loopy. I might've been embarrassed he'd seen the penis cake, but the little hint of a grin was enough to set me on fire inside. I quickly took my phone back and tapped out my password.

"There. Look at whatever you need," I announced, remembering to throw a glare in Tracksuit's direction.

Tracksuit simply rolled his eyes and crossed his arms again.

Sexy cop caught my eyes. "I can look at anything?"

The corner of his mouth hitched up again. My cheeks got even hotter. I shrugged and adjusted my purse on my shoulder. "I have nothing to hide."

He arched a brow and glanced down at my phone screen. "I'd say not," he murmured.

I twirled a lock of my hair around my finger, watching as he pulled up my texts and calls before handing my phone back to me. His eyes held the barest hint of a gleam, flicking down to my screen again as the cake penis reappeared when he closed out the list of calls.

"All I needed to see were your calls, texts and activity log. Entirely unnecessary to see anything else," he said.

The sound of his voice sent a shiver up my spine and heat unfurling in a wave through my body. All I could manage was a nod.

Sexy cop glanced from Tracksuit to me. "There's no evidence her phone was in use. It's heavy traffic, and you were behind her, likely following too closely."

He paused and Tracksuit jumped in.

"That's bullshit. I know…"

I temporarily forgot my speechless state. Aside from being an obnoxious jerk, Tracksuit sadly reminded me of my last boss. He had the same cocky attitude. My last boss had pretty much ruined my life. Mistake number one: never date your boss. That itself was bad enough, but the worst part was I didn't actually know he was married. How I missed that massively relevant detail, I didn't know. Anyway, in short, it blew up my life, and Tracksuit reminded me of him.

"You fucking asshole! It's *not* bullshit. I wasn't on my phone. You bumped into me. Shut up and deal…"

Sexy cop put his hand on my arm, effectively ending my tirade. Just the feel of his hand on me made me hot all over and snapped me out of my focus on Tracksuit. I glanced over at him. The moment I met his eyes, I discovered I could happily stare at him all day.

"Yes?"

"Entirely unnecessary to argue," he said, that slightly haughty tone of his sending my belly in a spinning flip.

I scrambled my thoughts together when he arched a brow, making me quite aware I was staring dumbly at him. "Right. So what now? My bumper's dented," I said, pointing to the crushed corner of said bumper. I drove a small, bright blue hatchback that had honestly seen better days, but I was rather attached to it. My little car had seen me through some rough years.

Sexy cop's eyes glanced to my car and back to me. "I'll write a citation, and you'll follow up with your insurance company," he said simply.

All very logical. I nodded, and he let go of my arm. Tracksuit seemed to have decided it wasn't worth arguing and leaned against his car, staring into traffic.

Sexy cop stepped away and responded to the voice crackling in the radio mounted on his shoulder. In short order, he wrote up a citation while I exchanged insurance information with Tracksuit.

Tracksuit drove away, still throwing glares at me. I ignored him and rounded the back of my car, only then noticing I had a flat tire.

I spun back and almost collided with sexy cop. My mouth went dry when I met his gaze. Sweet hell. He was so damn hot, it wasn't fair.

Somehow I managed to form words. "I have a flat tire."

It was a damn miracle I didn't melt into a puddle at his feet.

Chapter Two

FINN

I stared at the woman standing before me, my eyes landing on a bright streak of purple in her hair. The purple stood out amidst the rich brown of her glossy dark hair. Ever since I'd laid eyes on her, I'd had a bloody hard time focusing. She was fucking beautiful, and if my cock had its way, I'd stare at her all day. Actually, I'd do far more than stare.

Dispatch had reported her information before I even arrived on the scene, so I knew her to be Jana Sparks. She had a squeaky clean driving record.

My first problem had been solved. By some miracle, I'd gotten her to stop arguing with the cocky prick who tried to blame their fender bender on her. My second problem was I could hardly stop looking at her and would quite happily toss her into my patrol car and drive away with her. Her wide blue eyes, fair skin and wild hair were mesmerizing. To say she wasn't my usual type would be a massive understatement. My ex had been what I'd call a classic beauty—blonde hair, blue eyes, always impeccably dressed and with a polite demeanor. Nothing like this brash woman standing before me, ready to argue over a citation. Her brightly streaked hair lent her a whimsical touch. She had curves for days and a boldness to her that hit me right in the gut, or rather my cock.

She crossed her arms and tapped her foot, drawing my gaze down. My willful eyes took a leisurely detour, absorbing the way her breasts pulled her blouse tight, and the way her hips flared out and flowed into curvy legs. She wore a fitted white blouse over a gray skirt. At a glance, her outfit was perfectly respectable. Yet, somehow on her, it made me crazy. Even the coffee stains were endearing—I surmised she'd spilled coffee when her car got bumped. When she huffed, I glanced up and recalled she'd just said something.

"My apologies. Come again?"

She spun her phone in her hand, reminding me she had a picture of a cake penis on the screen. I had to admit, whoever made that cake had some serious skill. For a moment, I'd thought it was real, but then I'd seen the gleam of the flesh-colored icing.

She sighed rather dramatically, her eyes flicking to the corner of her crumpled bumper. "I have a flat tire," she said.

Her voice had a husky quality to it, only adding to the utter distraction she presented.

"I'll make arrangements for a tow truck for you. Do you need a ride somewhere?" I asked.

This was what I would ask anyone in this particular situation, yet it didn't escape my attention that this would offer me some time alone with her.

Her gorgeous blue eyes widened. "You'll give me a ride?"

She seemed surprised by the simple suggestion.

"If you need one, yes. We're in the middle of heavy traffic," I said, stating that rather obvious point.

Jana huffed and brushed a lock of purple hair behind her ear. "Well, of course. If you'll give me a ride, I'll take a ride. I was on my way to work, so I don't really have time to follow the tow truck."

We happened to be on I-5 in Seattle, one of the busiest

highways in the area. It was far too busy for a tire change on the side of the overpass, not to mention it appeared her tire rim had been dented in the fender bender.

She leaned her hips against her car and crossed her arms. I interpreted that as a sign she was willing to wait. I slipped out my cell phone and tapped dispatch.

"Hey Rosie," I said as soon as her voice crackled in my radio. "Can you call a tow company for me?"

Rosie was all business and ever efficient. "Got it. Let me confirm your location."

She quickly recited exactly where we were. "Correct," I replied.

The radio went silent and then crackled again. "They said they'd be there in about 15 minutes."

I looked back at Jana, thinking her name suited her quite perfectly. She still had her arms crossed, and she looked rather put out by the entire thing. I met her annoyed gaze, puzzled by the fact I enjoyed how riled up she was.

"Shall we wait in my car?" I offered.

Her eyes lit up. "Sure! I've never been in a cop car. Can I sit in the front?"

I bit back the urge to grin. "Of course."

She pushed her hips off of her car, and I gestured for her to walk ahead of me. Mistake. I hadn't seen the sweet curve of her bottom from behind, and it only made my cock harder. I watched her hips swing as she walked ahead of me. She reached for the door handle only to sigh elaborately when it didn't open for her.

That time, I didn't bother not to chuckle. "You didn't think it would just open, did you? It automatically locks the second I'm more than a foot away," I explained.

She rolled her eyes and waited while I tapped my key fob and unlocked it for her, opening the door to gesture her in. As her legs swung inside, I caught a glimpse of bright blue silk between her thighs. Fuck me.

I shut the door a little too quickly and walked around the

back of the car, willing my mind not to think about her hot, little body. She was short and curvy. I didn't know what it was about this woman between her wild hair, her proper clothes, and her attitude, but she was like a straight shot of delectable. I wanted her. I couldn't help but think how hot she would look with that skirt up around her waist in the back of my car. In fact, I was thinking it would be ideal for her hands to be curled over the back of the seat while I fucked her from behind.

Just the other day, we had a workshop on ethics. I knew perfectly well I wasn't supposed to want to fuck a woman whose fender bender I'd responded to, yet my body didn't give a damn about ethics. I usually found our annual ethics workshops boring as hell. But then, I'd never, ever wanted to fuck anyone I crossed paths with in my official role as a police officer for the City of Seattle. I paused for a moment when I got to the back of my car. I needlessly glanced at my phone and checked my email. I couldn't stand back here forever though. I slipped my phone back into my shirt pocket and rounded the car, climbing into the driver's seat.

Jana's eyes were curious and soaking in everything. My police cruiser had a small computer tablet in between the seats and various gadgets on the dash. Her wide blue eyes landed on me.

"Wow. You have all kinds of stuff in here. This is awesome. Can you turn on your siren?" she asked.

I stared at her, willing my cock down. "Usually kids ask that," I managed.

I gave into the urge to grin when she smiled. Her smile hit me right in my gut, and blood shot to my groin. Her mouth was wide and mobile, her lips plump. She had a refreshing quality of lightness and mischief to her. She was the first woman I'd met in years that elicited much of anything from me.

"What's a British guy doing here in Seattle as a cop?" she asked.

That was a bloody good question. I had a practiced answer. "I moved here during university, and I stayed."

What I didn't offer was that in university, I'd fallen in love and gotten engaged. I'd stayed engaged for far too long and then three days before the wedding, my fiancée dumped me. Said fiancée was the reason I had stayed in Seattle after university. Kristen hadn't wanted to move away from Seattle, and I'd fancied myself in love with her. I'd ended up in law enforcement, although that hadn't been the plan. Rather, I'd been a football star in university. Excuse me, soccer. I'd been on track to likely land a position as a professional player when I got badly injured in a car accident. I fully recovered from my injuries, but by then it was too late to get back into the game at the pro level. I turned to my second interest and became a police officer.

My answer to Jana was a quite truncated version of why I truly stayed in Seattle. I had a life here now and friends. My family was far away in London. My canceled wedding had been years ago, and I was staring down 32 now. I was rather cynical about the whole thing. I had thought I loved Kristen, and the way she'd broken up with me had stung. Even better, she shagged one of my former friends from university. I'd had little to no interest in dating since then and only sought out the most casual of encounters.

Jana cocked her head to the side. "Really? Is Seattle better than Britain?"

I stared at her for a moment, pondering her question. I liked Seattle, and I enjoyed living in the States. Yet, I kept meaning to move back to London. I hadn't gotten around to it, if only because life kept me busy. That was my only excuse.

To her I simply said, "Seattle's a fair city. You know how it goes. You move somewhere and then you stay sometimes."

I looked over at Jana who sat beside me—bright, funny, bold and brash—and wondered why she lit a spark inside of me. At my rather basic answer, she nodded.

"Ah, okay. Quite simple really."

She shifted her legs, and my eyes automatically flicked down. I wanted another glimpse of that blue silk between her thighs, actually I wanted quite a bit more.

My eyes traveled up, willfully lingering on the shadowed valley between her breasts. Bloody hell. She was so fucking tempting. Thank fuck I was seated with the small monitor mounted between us. It shielded her view of my lap. Otherwise, it would be difficult to hide the fact that I was hard as a rock.

Jana's eyes landed on the handcuffs hanging from a hook in between the seats.

"Do you ever have people in the front seat?" she asked.

She reached for the cuffs, lifting them up and circling them in her hands. The vision that flashed in my mind was absolutely not appropriate. It was her, cuffed on my bed with her hands over her head. Every inch of her that I'd never seen bare for me and that wild dark hair with purple streaks a splash of color against my cream colored sheets.

I swallowed, nudging the image out of my mind and forcing myself to respond to her question.

"Not usually. If someone needs to be cuffed, they're in the back," I explained, gesturing toward the steel screen behind us that separated the front from the back. I considered that I probably should've put her in the back. She was a handful. I held my hand out.

"What?" she asked with a sly smile.

"Hand over the cuffs." I had to fight the urge to smile.

"I'm not gonna do anything with them. That shouldn't be a problem, right?"

I rolled my eyes, waving my fingers. "Hand them over," I repeated.

With an elaborate sigh, she did. I hooked them on my belt out of her reach.

Chapter Three

JANA

Oh. My. God. He was the hottest cop ever, and I didn't even know his name yet. I needed to know.

"What's your name?" I asked, getting right to the point.

He narrowed his deep blue eyes, his mouth hitching up at the corner. Wow. He was just delicious. I wanted to lick him all over. It was probably completely inappropriate for me to be lusting after a cop, but I couldn't bring myself to care. I wished there wasn't all the stuff in between us because I wanted to climb right over the console and ride him. Preferably with his uniform on. He was so hot in his blue uniform with his wide shoulders and chest filling it out quite nicely. I'd gotten a good look at his tight ass when he walked to his car to write up the citation for the jerk who bumped into me.

When I handed the cuffs over, his fingers brushed against mine, and a hot jolt of electricity shot through me. I knew he felt it too because I saw his nostrils flare.

You need to stop this. What is it with you and wanting to fuck men you're not supposed to want to fuck? For example, the cop who just responded to your fender bender.

I didn't know what it was with me. I had an inconvenient weakness for guys I wasn't supposed to want. It hadn't been a problem for a while. Not since my last boss, who I got naughty with all over the office by the way. I loved office sex. The fun and games with my former boss came to a screeching halt when I learned he was married. There was naughty and then there was absolutely not okay. Screwing around with someone who was married fell in the *absolutely not okay* category. Not only had I been mortified and embarrassed, I was tarnished as the 'other woman' and felt awful, just awful, about it. I lost my job and my reputation all at once.

The whole mess had happened when my mom was dying from cancer. It was safe to say it was a fiasco. I thought it had permanently cured me of my inconvenient attraction to men I shouldn't want. Definitely not.

With sexy cop sitting here across for me—oh my wow! I wanted him like I'd never wanted anybody. Just thinking about what we could do here in his car made me squirm in my seat. My panties were wet and had been ever since he climbed in the car beside me.

"Finn Connors," he said, reminding me I'd actually asked him his name.

"Should I call you Officer Connors or Officer Finn?"

I couldn't help but grin because this was fun. His nostrils flared again, and I wished like hell that damn console thing and computer wasn't in between us. I wanted to know if he was hard because I was wet, so wet it was a problem.

"Technically, it would be Sergeant Finn, but you can just call me Finn," he said in that hot British accent.

It sent my belly into a tailspin of flutters. My best friend Zoe was married to a British guy. Zoe was also technically my boss. She was one of only a few friends who reached out after my reputation went up in flames over the affair I hadn't known was an affair. Ethan Walsh, Zoe's husband, was a hot British soccer player from the Seattle Stars. He totally fell for her when she was his attorney. I'd thought all the British guys in Seattle were snapped up after that. Apparently not. I took it as a sign. I wanted to have Finn, and I would. I just didn't know how exactly I would go about getting him.

"Sergeant Finn. That's better than just Finn."

His grin widened, and he shook his head slowly.

"Just call me Finn," he repeated.

I rolled my eyes. "Why not Sergeant Finn?"

He chuckled and looked away from me, giving me an excellent view of his profile. Dear God. The man should've been a model. He had that whole sculpted thing going on with his cheekbones and jaw.

"We might as well get to know each other. My name is Jana," I said, if only because I wanted him to look at me again.

Finn turned back just as I held my hand out. He actually reached over and shook my hand. It was awesome. That little zing from when he took the handcuffs from me was nothing compared to this. His touch was a hot jolt straight to my core. His hand was warm and strong. I could feel the slightly calloused surface of his palm around mine, and I wanted to feel it all over my body.

I didn't want to let go. His name made it even worse. It was so sexy, and it suited him perfectly. As I sat there staring at him, thinking I didn't want to let go of his hand, lights flashed in his rear view mirror. The tow truck was here. With that half grin of his, I could hardly look away. He slowly released my hand and started to turn to open his door.

My words tumbled out. "Have dinner with me."

He swung back quickly, his deep blue gaze sending a shiver down my spine.

"Pardon?"

His voice sent goose bumps prickling over my skin.

"Have dinner with me," I repeated.

He stared at me and then shook his head slowly. "Ms.

Sparks," he began, just now becoming formal. "I'm a police officer. At the moment, I just responded to the scene of your accident. It wouldn't do for me to plan to go out to dinner with you."

"Okay, maybe not now, but later."

I was disappointed, quite disappointed actually. He grinned again and shook his head as he climbed out of the car, never replying to my last comment.

Sergeant Finn—I just had to call him that in my mind— dropped me off at the office. I was disappointed at how short our drive was. By the time the tow truck driver dealt with my car and we had seen him off with a plan for me to go pick it up at the end of the day, Finn drove me to the office in minutes. He'd been busy responding to a call on the radio, so I hadn't even had a chance to flirt with him on the way there. Instead, I had texted Zoe to explain why I was late. I pushed through the door into the office, glancing around, relieved to find no one waiting in the reception area. I was a paralegal and receptionist for Zoe Walsh. She was a hotshot criminal defense attorney. We'd started law school together. I'd dropped out when my mom got breast cancer. I'd managed to scrabble together the funds to finish up my paralegal requirements, but I'd never been able to finish law school. Money and life got in the way.

While I was busy taking care of my mother, I landed a job as a paralegal at a high-end law firm. It had been a great job for my resume. I should've had enough sense not to get tangled up with my boss, but I had and, well, you already know that story. Needless to say, I lost my job. It was a large, well known law firm, and my reputation had taken a hit. Not too long after that, my mother passed away, which had been incredibly hard for me. We'd been close, and I still missed her.

Zoe, good friend that she was, reached out to me when she started her practice and offered me a position as a paralegal for her. She was still encouraging me to return to law school and finish up my classes, so I could actually get my law degree. I kept telling myself I would, but it hadn't happened yet. Working with Zoe was a pleasure. She couldn't afford to pay me as well as my old job had, but even before everything had blown up there, it hadn't been the most pleasant place to work. Being nice didn't fit in well with the cutthroat competitiveness fostered there.

Here it was just Zoe and me. I loved working with her and had enormous respect for her. She also let me do my job as I saw fit. Her office door was closed when I arrived. I knew she had a meeting, so I swung behind the desk of my little kingdom as I called it. I handled all the reception and paralegal duties, so I was the face everybody saw when they first came in the door. I had a small office behind the reception desk, but I rarely went there unless I needed to speak privately with someone.

With nothing other than Finn on my mind—his hard, hot body, his gorgeous eyes, and his mouth made for sin—I sat down at my desk and got to work. I caught up on voice messages, got through my email and then began working on a few draft legal filings for Zoe to review later. Around lunchtime, the client she'd been meeting with exited the office. Zoe came out front, leaning her hips against my desk.

Zoe was gorgeous with beautiful auburn hair, bright hazel eyes and fair skin. She was also willowy and somehow managed to have curves at the same time. When I first met her in college, I'd been struck by how oblivious she seemed to how beautiful she was. After I got to know her, I learned she'd been rather awkward looking all through high school, towering over most of the guys. She still towered over some of them now, but she'd definitely grown into her beauty. She'd gotten married only a year or so ago to Ethan Walsh, soccer star for the Seattle Stars. Ethan was eye candy for most women, so we still laughed about the whole thing.

I was more than happy for Zoe because Ethan adored her. I knew by most standards, she wasn't a typical woman. She was brilliant, dedicated to her career and not one be wowed easily. Ethan had fallen for her, hook, line and sinker. He was currently trying to persuade her it was time for them to start planning a family, while Zoe was undecided if she was ready for that yet. She crossed her arms once the door clicked shut behind her client.

"God, I hate it when I end up agreeing to take a case for an idiot," she said with a sigh.

"Oh? So Carl Chambers isn't a great client?" I asked with a sly grin.

Zoe rolled her eyes. Hooking her foot on a chair across from my desk, she pulled it closer before sitting down.

"No. I keep trying to tell him that insider trading is a problem, and that they have a good case against him. If he had half a brain, he would settle. He's not seeing the light yet. I always tell people an attorney is only as good as the truth they tell their clients. I keep trying to tell him the truth, and he doesn't want to hear it."

"I warned you about him, but you love a challenge."

Zoe sighed again, picking up a pen on my desk and idly flipping it back-and-forth between her fingers. "You did, and I do like a challenge. But there's a challenge and then there's an annoying, stubborn client. Carl Chambers is that client."

"I warned you," I repeated. Because I had. I'd crossed paths with Carl at my last job. He burned through attorneys fast because of his stubbornness.

Zoe rolled her eyes. "I'll deal with him, but I should've listened to you. Anyway, what happened with your car?" she asked.

"Fender bender. No biggie. My bumper's crushed on one side, but that's not why I was so late. We had to wait for a tow truck because my tire rim also got bent, which gave me a flat tire. The police officer arranged for the tow truck. The repair shop said they'll have the bumper and my tire repaired by the end of the day. I was hoping you didn't mind dropping me off to pick it up later."

"Of course not. Nice of the police to call a tow truck for you."

I couldn't help but grin. I was rather shameless when it came to appreciating men.

"Oh, it was great. You're not gonna believe it, but the cop was a British guy. He went to university here and stayed. He's delicious."

Zoe leaned back in her chair and grinned. "Oh, you don't say? Let me guess. You asked him out for dinner?"

"I tried! He said no and said it wouldn't be proper. But I got his name, and I'm gonna look him up and call him again."

Zoe burst out laughing.

At that moment, the door pushed open and Zoe's husband Ethan stepped through. Ethan didn't do a thing for me, but I could definitely appreciate a handsome man, and man, oh man, was he ever handsome. He had honey blonde hair, green eyes, and a body to die for. I didn't suppose one could be a professional soccer player and not have that. Throw in his endearing dimple, and plenty of women melted on sight. Zoe didn't melt, but she adored him.

Ethan stepped over and dropped a lingering kiss on the side of Zoe's neck. She blushed and swatted him away. He merely chuckled and sank down into the chair beside her. Glancing at me, he nudged his chin up. "Hello, Jana. How are you today?"

"Oh, I had a fender bender, and I got pulled over by a hot British cop," I announced.

Ethan grinned while Zoe rolled her eyes.

"What are the chances of that?" she mused, glancing to Ethan.

He lifted one shoulder in a lazy shrug. "No idea, but I happen to know a British cop though."

"Of course you do, you're from London," Zoe said.

"Luv, I know one here," he said, throwing a teasing grin her way.

Zoe wasn't easily ruffled, but Ethan had her number. It annoyed her to no end he flirted just by opening his mouth.

"Really? How many British cops could there be in Seattle?" I asked.

"Well, Finn Connors is the only one I know, and the only reason I know him is he used to play football in university. He was on his way to the pros when he got in a nasty car accident. By the time he recovered enough to play again, it was almost two years later."

"Are you serious?" I asked, knowing this had to be the same Finn and grappling to absorb this information. His life had been spun off track in stunning fashion.

"Completely serious. Finn was a brilliant playmaker, one of the best, and probably would've been signed to a great team. I don't know all the details, but he broke both of his ankles in that accident. Took a bloody long time for him to recover. He might've been able to make a go for it, but a year and a half passed. He wasn't eligible to play for university anymore and that was it. Finn's a good bloke. I've had a few beers with him here and there when we run into each other."

My mind conjured up that delicious image of Finn. No wonder he was in such good shape. He was an ex soccer player. I wondered what it was like for him to see a career like that go up in smoke. It only made me all the more curious about him.

I looked over at Ethan. "So do you ever see him?" I asked. "I've never even heard you mention him."

Zoe rolled her eyes, casting a glance toward Ethan. "Jana thinks he's hot," she offered in explanation. "That's why she's being so nosy."

Ethan cracked a grin. "Well, I shan't say I think he's hot,

but I can imagine you would. He was engaged for a bit. That's why he stayed in the States. Anyway, she dumped him a few days before the wedding. It was bloody ugly. I don't know Finn well enough to know how it went, but rumor had it he was pretty broken up over it. I'm surprised he's still around in Seattle."

I instantly wanted to beat up the nameless woman who dumped Finn. What foolish woman would dump a man like him? Aside from the fact he was so hot I wanted to eat him up, he seemed quite nice. I didn't appreciate it when nice people got shafted.

"So do you ever see him?" I repeated.

Ethan shook his head. "Not much."

I leaned back in my chair with a sigh. I'd been hoping I had an opening with him. No such luck. Fine.

Zoe merely shook her head. "I'm sure you'll track him down," she said as she stood from her chair.

Ethan stood with her, slipped his arm around her waist and pulled her right up against his side. He was rather handsy with her, and I loved it because it meant he adored her. They left to go to lunch, and I hopped on my computer, determined to see if I could scout down Finn Connors.

Chapter Four

FINN

Roughly a week after my encounter with the delectable Jana, I pushed through the door into Desert Isle Coffee, one of the coffee shops I frequented around Seattle. Truth be told, Jana had been in and out of my thoughts all week. As far as fantasies went, she was making herself at home in my brain. Ever since Kristen and I broke up, I'd been rather cynical about even the idea of dating. It's not that I was celibate. I wasn't that foolish, but I definitely kept things casual as far as dating went. In my encounters through the course of my job and life, Jana held the distinction of being the one and only woman I couldn't stop thinking about.

I kept wondering if I should've answered differently when she tried to get me to go out to dinner with her. I would've loved to have dinner with her, and I would love to do more than simply fantasize about her delicious curves. I stood in line, brushing my hand over my damp hair. It was rainy out, not a surprise for Seattle. I was just finishing up an overnight shift. A buddy needed coverage, so I'd taken his shift and was headed straight into a day shift now. I worked more than I probably should, but it was what it was. All in all, given that I hadn't gotten to go into my dream career, I was fairly happy with my job. When I was a lad in London, I had two career paths in mind—either a police officer, or a football player. Since the car accident had taken the option of professional sports away from me, I was content to be a police officer.

As I waited in line, I felt someone tap me on the shoulder. I glanced behind me to see Jana. The second my eyes landed on her, a jolt of need hit me. Bloody hell. Her mere presence was a straight shot of lust in my veins. Her hair had an added layer of pink streaks mingling in with the purple streaks and rich mahogany color. Her hair was damp, and her blue eyes were bright. She smiled widely when I saw her.

"I'm so happy I found you!" she exclaimed.

Her smile was irresistible. My body tightened and my cock twitched.

"Hello, Jana," I said with a nod. "How are you?"

"I'm great now. I've been trying to find you," she said, stepping closer to me and speaking in a conspiratorial tone.

I leaned down, her scent drifting up to me. She smelled like strawberries, which suited her perfectly somehow.

"You've been trying to find me?" I asked, my voice low.

She nodded, her dangly silver earrings swinging with the motion of her head. "Yes. Now that we're done with the fender bender, you're just a cop, so we can have dinner."

She said this as if fully expecting me to go along with it. I surprised myself by doing just that.

"I suppose we can. When shall we have dinner?"

Her smile widened, and my cock twitched again. Bloody hell. She just did it for me, and I couldn't figure out why for the life of me. She was wild, brash, funny and endearing. Aside from the fact that my body obviously had an opinion on the matter, she was fun. I couldn't say I'd spent much time with her, but every minute of it had been amusing.

Jana angled her head to the side, twirling a pink lock of hair around her finger and tapping her other index finger on her chin. "Well, it's Thursday. How about tomorrow night because then it'll be Friday?"

"Friday does follow Thursday. Every week," I replied.

She grinned even wider and giggled. "It does. Glad you noticed. So what do you say? Dinner tomorrow? I'll pick you up," she offered.

"No, I'll pick you up," I countered.

I couldn't say I was thinking about a word I was saying.

She sighed elaborately. "Okay, can you pick me up in your cop car?"

I shook my head, fighting the urge to laugh aloud. "No, that's for business."

"We can pretend you're arresting me and call it business," she added brightly.

I couldn't hold back my laugh any longer. "It's not business. I'll pick you up in my regular car. Tell me where."

She pulled her phone out of her pocket. "Tell me your number. Your personal number," she said with an arch of her brow and a sly smile. "I'll text you my number and my address. You'll know exactly where to find me. Since you're driving, I'll pick the time and place."

I shrugged, still rather disbelieving I was going along with this entire exchange, but I couldn't seem to kick my usual cynical brain in gear.

"Fair enough. Tell me when and where."

"Number first, please."

I quickly recited it, and she tapped it into her screen. Then, she nudged me in the back of my leg with her knee. My confusion must've shown on my face.

"It's your turn," she explained.

Bloody hell. Jana had me so enraptured, I had forgotten I was even in line, or where we were. I'd also forgotten the fact that I was damn tired and headed into a long shift. I spun around quickly and stepped to the counter, ordering my coffee and telling the cashier that I would also cover Jana's. I wanted to sit down and enjoy a cup of coffee with her, but I knew that was dangerous. I couldn't help but chuckle at myself. It was bad enough I'd agreed to have dinner with her.

After we respectively got our coffees, I was standing beside her while she added a dash of cream to hers.

"Reply to my text," she said, rather out of the blue.

I slipped my phone out and saw her message.

It's Jana!

I almost spewed my coffee all over the place when I saw what she sent next. She'd forwarded the photo of the penis cake.

When I looked up, she looked so pleased with herself all I could do was shake my head. "I noticed that before. Did you make it?"

She grinned and shook her head. "Nope, but it makes me laugh. I thought you might like to laugh too."

While her words were light, the sentiment struck a chord in me. She genuinely seemed to want to give me a reason to smile. I shifted my shoulders, uncertain of what to make of that.

"Laughing is good," I said, rather inanely.

Giving myself a shake, I tried to focus. "So where and when?"

"I'll text you later. It'll be a surprise."

My radio conveniently crackled, putting out a call for a response to a nearby location.

Jana leaned over, whispering in my ear. "Can I go with you?"

I looked to her, fighting the urge to grin and instantly losing the battle. I managed to shake my head. "No, you can't. Text me the details, and I'll see you tomorrow."

At that, I grabbed my coffee. As I turned away, she

leaned up and kissed me on the cheek. That little point of contact shot like a bolt of lightning through my body.

Later that afternoon, I pulled up behind yet another fender bender, this one on a downtown side street in Seattle. I handled patrol duty and forensic investigations for domestic violence cases. As the sergeant for my unit, I enjoyed the flexibility and variety. As I stepped out of my car, my mind flashed back to the last fender bender I'd handled. I'd never have expected responding to a fender bender would lead to days of fantasies. Jana's presence made that minor incident memorable. She was seared into my brain. This accident was more typical. This involved two male drivers arguing. There was nothing amusing about it, no brash, endearing woman with pink and purple hair to make my day.

I'd glanced at her penis cake several times today, and sure enough, it was impossible to see without laughing. I was relieved I'd had enough sense not to give her my work contact. I went through the usuals to deal with the accident. I ended up writing up both men because the guy who got hit from behind actually threatened to punch the other guy. Fun afternoon.

I strolled into the station later, ready to finish up my second shift. I was weary and looking forward to a good night's sleep. I took care of things in the computer system quickly and then headed in to the locker room to leave my gear. Eli Phillips was lounging in the kitchen, nursing a cup of coffee and idly flipping through the paper. I slipped into the chair across from him and glanced over.

"How's it going, mate?" I asked.

Eli looked up and flashed a quick grin. His blue eyes crinkled at the corners as he ran a hand through his dark brown hair. "Eh, boring day. You?"

I shrugged. My reply was more automatic than anything else. "Same. Nothing remarkable."

Unless I counted Jana. I wasn't going to get into Jana with Eli.

"How's Beth?" I asked, referring to Eli's longtime girlfriend.

Eli drummed his fingers on the table and took a gulp of his coffee before replying. "We broke up actually."

"Oh?"

I was surprised to hear this. Eli was what I thought of as an All-American guy. He was clean-cut and handsome. He enjoyed watching sports and loved hamburgers and fries. He was slightly more evolved than the stereotype. He was quite bright and had tested into the forensic unit straight out of the police academy. He'd seemed more than content to carry-on dating Beth. In fact, I'd expected them to be engaged any day now and happily married soon. At my surprised look, he ran a hand through his hair again and leaned back in his chair.

"Why does everybody look so surprised?" he asked.

I studied him for a moment. "I suppose because you two have been living together for a few years, and you seemed as happy as anyone."

Eli shrugged. "Yeah I guess we seemed like that," he finally said.

"You doing okay?"

He drained his coffee before standing and stepping to the counter for a refill. He quickly filled another cup for himself and glanced to me. "Want some?"

At my nod, he filled another cup before returning to the table. He slid one coffee across to me. Break room coffee here was nothing to write home about, but it was probably better than most. Seattle was known as a hub for coffee, being home to Starbucks and many other local shops, a few of which provided us with an endless supply of good coffee. It depended on who made it as to how good it was.

I took a swallow and was heartened to discover that whoever had passed by to make this pot of coffee knew what the hell they were doing. It was damn good.

I glanced to Eli. "You make this?"

He flashed a grin and winked. "Of course."

"So anyway, you doing okay, mate?" I repeated my question.

He nodded, drumming his fingertips on the table again. "Yeah. I'm not all broken up about it, which is honestly why I broke up with her in the first place."

I cocked my head to the side. "What do you mean?"

"I don't know. We were just drifting along. There was never a huge spark with her. I don't know if I want to settle down, or if I want a family. She was making all kinds of noises about it, and I didn't want more. If I'm gonna put time and energy into something, it should be with someone where I'm damn upset if we break up."

"How did this come about?" I asked.

"Actually, she got pissed off about something. Not even a big deal. Then, she said something about how I wouldn't even care if she broke up with me." He paused for a sip of coffee before continuing. "I thought about it, and it's not that I don't care. I do, but she was right. I wouldn't have been devastated, and I'm not."

"How's Beth doing?"

He was quiet for a beat. "I think she's okay. Her pride took a hit, but honestly she's not all broken up over it either. I wish her the best, and I imagine we'll be able to be friends when the dust settles."

I took another swallow of my coffee and leaned back in my chair. We were quiet for a few moments, both of us respectively nursing our coffees.

Eli spoke again, his voice startling me out of my reverie about Jana. Because, honestly, that's the only place my mind went when I had a spare moment this past week. She'd pretty much planted herself in my brain like a flag on the moon.

"Were you all broken up when you and Kristen ended things?" he asked.

I eyed him and laughed softly, a tinge of bitterness in it. "I can't say our break up was mutual," I offered.

He rolled his eyes. "True, but still?"

I pondered his question and what I knew of love at that time in my life. I had believed myself in love with Kristen. But we were young. Hell, we'd met in university. Now that I was staring down 32, my early 20's felt like adolescence almost. I took a breath and let it out.

"It's fair to say I was more upset than you are right now. Looking back, what pissed me off about it was the way it played out. I think she knew much sooner that she wanted things to end. She could've said something then instead of stringing me along," I finally said.

What I didn't say aloud was what I'd contemplated many times. Things began to feel different with her after my car accident. We had started dating when I was on a full ride scholarship at the University of Washington for soccer. She loved the games and the life that went with it. I had my car accident and everything shifted. Don't get me wrong, she was there for me. She helped afterwards with my recovery, carting me to and from appointments when I couldn't drive for a little while and the like. But she had cooled. Thinking back, she probably didn't know what to do because it was uncomfortable to think she might've fallen for me mostly because of the lifestyle I might have offered her in the future.

What she didn't know was I had plenty of money. I had enough that I didn't have to do what I was choosing to do right now. I knew a life without something meaningful would drive me bloody mad, so I'd chosen to go into the police academy. My father ran a very successful banking firm in London. Kristen knew that, although I didn't know that she ever knew quite how much money my family had. My parents lived a fairly simple life. Oh, they were comfortable, but they weren't ostentatious. I'd been raised in the typical British fashion where you didn't talk about money and you didn't flaunt it. I certainly didn't choose to enlighten her on my status after my accident. My trust fund wouldn't be available to me until after I turned thirty-five. I had figured—wisely, in hindsight—money wasn't something I wanted anyone to calculate into a relationship with me.

As my thoughts circled back to Eli's question, I shrugged. "I think so, but loving someone when you're in your early twenties and loving someone now are two very different things."

He nodded and then arched a brow. "How would you know about loving someone now?" he asked with a chuckle.

"Touché, mate. Excellent question."

Jana again sauntered through my thoughts.

"You seeing anyone?" he asked.

My automatic answer was no. I considered whether to share my date for tomorrow with Jana, yet that didn't mean I was seeing her. So I shook my head and took a gulp of coffee. Our conversation was interrupted by another few blokes coming into the break room.

I made my way out to my car, finally looking forward to a good night's sleep. I paused to check my phone when it buzzed in my pocket, reminding me I had yet to read a text that came in earlier. Outside of my family and a few friends here, I wasn't much for texting. My mother would send me polite updates on the weather and ask me how I was doing. Friends here would check in to confirm what time I was stopping by and the like. It was fair to say I didn't expect anything eventful in the form of a text.

I glanced down to see a message from Jana.

43 Castle St.

My apartment is upstairs.

6 o'clock

Simple enough. But then came the picture. This was another angle of the penis cake I'd glimpsed on her phone, this one standing straight up on the table. I laughed so hard, I almost cried. When I finally caught my breath, I glanced around, realizing I was sitting alone in my car laughing my bloody arse off at a picture of a penis cake. I leaned back in my seat, still smiling. How Jana knew I could use more laughter in my life, I didn't know. She was this bright light of bubbly joy...and sexy as hell to boot. Her face appeared in my mind with her dark hair and bright streaks of color, her wide blue eyes, and her slightly lopsided mouth. Her lips were plump and pink, so damn tempting.

I put my car in gear and headed home. It was only after I got home that I realized I'd yet to even reply to Jana's text. I paused before I went into my apartment and tapped out a reply.

I'll be there. 6 o'clock.

I didn't even know how to reply to the penis cake.

I lived in a townhouse overlooking Puget Sound. It was a nice residential neighborhood with a beautiful view. I'd moved here after Kristen and I broke up. My footsteps echoed as I walked across the hardwood flooring after stepping inside. It was a lovely townhouse. I probably didn't do it justice. The décor was simple. My younger sister had come to visit after I moved. Any and all warm touches were solely her doing. The townhouse had hardwood floors and high ceilings. Beyond the entryway, there was a kitchen to the right through a small archway and then it opened out into the living room. The windows offered a view of Puget Sound in the distance. A love seat and a matching couch of sage green with a large ottoman were in the center of the living room. My sister Sarah had purchased brightly colored throw rugs that were scattered about the room.

A hallway led to three bedrooms. It was completely illogical for me to have a three bedroom townhouse, but I hadn't been thinking particularly clearly when I moved here. I kicked my shoes off and dropped my keys in a small blown glass bowl on a table just outside the kitchen. The sound echoed in the empty townhouse. I didn't think much about the fact that I lived alone. Yet, just now, the reality of it hit me right in the gut. I glanced around, imagining what it would be like for Jana to be here. I gave myself a shake. I didn't know what the hell I was thinking. I could have dinner with her, and I could have sex with her, but hoping for more was crazy.

Chapter Five

FINN

The following evening, I turned onto Castle Street, scanning the road for Jana's place. It had been an unusually clear day, and the sun was setting, casting soft rays of gold over Seattle. My gaze landed on a bungalow style house. The downstairs had a wide porch. When I saw the stairs on the side of the house, I assumed they led to her place per her text that she lived upstairs. Even the stairs had Jana's whimsical touch. Each stair had a hand-painted flower in the center of the tread. I knocked on the door, ignoring the tightening of my body.

I had dated here and there, rather frequently actually. Yet, I hadn't seen anyone where I felt this kind of anticipation. In seconds, Jana swung the door open. One look at her and lust hit me like lightning. Her hair was pulled up into a knot with loose tendrils falling around her face. She wore dangly silver earrings that swung when she moved. She wore no make up other than a dash of pink lipstick. Her lips were glossy and so tempting, it was all I could do not to kiss her right then and there.

"Hi Finn! Come in, come in," she said with a wide smile, gesturing for me to follow her inside.

I entered into one large, expansive room. It was a living room, kitchen, and dining room all in one. The kitchen was on one side with an island that faced the rest of the room. A round wooden table was situated near the island with chairs. The living room had a curved sofa with brightly colored rugs scattered on the hardwood floor. Plants abounded everywhere, making the space feel alive and warm. Seeing bright red ribbons twining around the windows with holiday lights reminded me December was days away.

Jana wore a stretchy black skirt that hugged her lush bottom with black knit thigh-high leggings. Atop that, she wore a loose blouse that swung with her hips as she moved. When she spun back to face me, the hem twirled slightly. The blouse scooped down just above her breasts with a tiny bow. The moment my eyes landed on that tie, I wanted to undo it. Preferably with my teeth. The fabric was slightly sheer. Not sheer enough to see anything, just sheer enough to drive me crazy. A pair of black cowboy boots finished off her ensemble, which suited her perfectly. Bracelets jingled on her wrist as she paused to pet a large gray cat.

"This is Smokey," she announced. "He's not the friendliest guy."

Great. An unfriendly cat. Our family cat when I was young had been best known for the scratches he inflicted upon us. I simply nodded. Before I had a chance to say anything else, Smokey leapt from his perch on the back of the couch toward me. In reflex, I caught him in my arms. For a moment, I thought he was going to hiss at me. He stared at me, his dark gray eyes scanning my face and then snuggled right up against my chest and promptly began to purr.

Chapter Six

JANA

I snagged my purse off the counter and spun around to look over at Finn. Smokey was snuggled up against his chest, purring like mad. I bit my lip to keep from laughing, if only because Finn looked flummoxed.

"Well, he likes you. That's a win," I finally said.

As if he'd suddenly discovered he'd made a fool of himself, Smokey bolted from Finn's arms and over to the windowsill. I hadn't realized I'd secretly hoped Finn would be wearing his uniform. I didn't know what that said about me, although I had to admit he looked just as delicious in his faded black jeans, his muscled legs outlined through the worn fabric, and his loose button-down shirt. His shoulders filled it out quite nicely. But then I imagined his shoulders filled out anything quite nicely. His straight dark hair was damp as if he had recently showered, and his blue eyes were bright.

I just loved that he seemed to have a semi-permanent 5 o'clock shadow. I wanted it to rough my skin just about anywhere. I watched as he glanced around my apartment, his eyes eventually making their way back to me. When they landed on me, it felt as if a flame lit the air between us. A prickle ran down my spine, and I almost shivered visibly.

I tried to recall the last time I'd been this attracted to a man. I'd be the first to admit I loved to flirt, and I loved to appreciate men. I hadn't dated much lately, hardly at all since everything went down with my ex-boss. Oh, that wasn't the only thing that sent my dating life down the tubes. It happened while my mom was dealing with breast cancer. After she lost the battle, I was depressed and broke because I was looking for a job. Dating had been the last thing on my mind. I'd gotten past the grief about my mom, yet I hadn't quite gotten back into the swing of dating. I still enjoyed flirting and appreciated a handsome man as much as the next woman. Whatever that meant.

I found it endlessly amusing that I happened to have an in with an entire team full of sexy guys with the Seattle Stars soccer team. With Zoe married to Ethan, I'd gotten to know his friends as well. Not a single one of those guys who had fan pages and the like did a thing for me. I could dispassionately appreciate them, yet nobody got to me like Finn.

Not since my ex-boss. I tried to recall if I'd been this attracted to my boss. It was hard to say. The illicit flavor of an office affair had turned me on like crazy, but of course I hadn't known he was married. It was difficult to have a clear recollection of what he meant to me, or how I felt. Pretty much impossible because all of it had been ruined when I learned he'd been married the whole time. It made me slightly sick to think about it after the fact. I felt so bad about the whole mess, I even went to apologize to his wife. They'd since divorced. She'd actually been rather gracious about it and had also told me I wasn't the only affair he had. Not that I thought I'd been special because I hadn't, but it just made me feel even worse for her.

Looking over at Finn, I suddenly blurted out a question. "Are you married?"

Finn's eyes widened. Ethan had seemed to think Finn

wasn't married, but Ethan also said they weren't close. After a beat, Finn shook his head, appearing puzzled by my question.

"No, certainly not."

Relief washed through me. "Sorry if that seemed weird."

His mouth hitched up at the corner, and he arched a brow in question. "It did seem a little strange. Do you usually worry about men you're going to dinner with being married?" he asked.

I took a breath and let it out with a sigh. "Well, no. I never did before, but I accidentally had an affair once. It's been a bit, but it was a disaster, and I felt awful," I explained.

Finn was standing by the island counter and leaned his elbow on it. "What do you mean you *accidentally* had an affair?" he asked.

"Oh, it sounds weird, but it was an accident because I didn't know he was married. He neglected to mention that really, really important detail. That's what I mean by *accidentally*."

His expression cleared. "Understood. Good to know that's not something you set out to do, I suppose."

I shook my head rapidly. "Oh no. It was awful, it ruined my reputation and everything." I waved a hand restlessly. "I'm glad you're not married. Shall we go?" I asked, striding to stand at his side, my cowboy boots echoing on the hardwood floor.

When I got close to him, I could smell him. Oh my God, he was just yummy. He had a crisp scent to him with a hint of rain. Was there anything about him that wasn't just nearly perfect?

I forgot I'd even asked him a question when he nodded.

Oh right, I'd asked him if he was ready to go.

"You never did tell me where we were going," he commented, the slightest grin curling the corner of his mouth.

My belly did a slow flip, as if on command. "Oh yes, it's a surprise," I managed, my voice a tad breathy.

He straightened, pushing away from the counter. "How am I supposed to know where to go if it's a surprise?" he asked, the other corner of his mouth curling up.

I wanted to kiss him so, so badly, but I was going to make myself wait. The anticipation was too delicious.

"Come on, let's go," I said, walking ahead of him.

He turned and followed behind me, catching up to open the door for me. He was quite polite, which didn't surprise me in the least. I led the way down the stairs, wondering if he experienced anything close to my reaction to him. When I reached the bottom of the stairs and glanced back up, my eyes landed conveniently on his cock. It was outlined by his worn jeans. Oh good. Considering that my panties were already wet, I was pleased to see his cock was plenty hard.

I didn't say a thing. I just looked up at him and smiled. We walked along the slate walkway around to the front of the house where I saw that he drove an all black sports car. It suited him quite perfectly. He opened the door for me and waited until I was seated before closing it and rounding the car.

Even his hands turned me on. He had a wrist hooked over the top of the steering wheel. A scar ran along the back of his hand, his fingers were long, strong and slightly battered. I imagined playing soccer had put his body to good use. I wanted to ask him about soccer, but then that would cue off the fact I'd been nosy about him, so I kept quiet.

Once he started the car, he looked at my direction. "Where to luv?"

Oh wow. My low belly clenched and heat radiated outward from my center. He could call me *luv* all day.

"We're going to a hibachi grill."

"And where would that be?" he countered with another one of his devastating half grins.

I wanted to keep asking questions, twenty questions

wouldn't be enough. I didn't even care what they were. I just wanted to hear him talk. I recited the address and then proceeded to pepper him with questions.

"So where in Britain did you live?"

"London," he said succinctly.

"I've never been to London, what's it like?"

One of his shoulders rose and fell in a small shrug. "It's London. Cities all share something I think. Simply in terms of the energy, the sheer mass of people. London is obviously quite different from Seattle. It's older, more stodgy, if you will. When I first came to the States, that was one of the things I liked about Seattle. It's fresh and young. As cities go, it's quite different from London in that sense, but there are things I miss about London. Though I must say, the food here is better. Can't say that perhaps for all of the States but definitely here in Seattle."

"Seattle takes food very seriously. It's why they call it a foodie city," I offered.

His low chuckle sent another shiver through me. I rubbed my thighs together, trying to quell the ache of need building between them. That's how delicious it was to just ride in the car with him. I wondered if I was crazy. I didn't really know what I was doing, but I liked Finn. A lot.

———

Noise hummed around us—snippets of conversation, chopping, the rhythmic sound of grilling—while I looked to Finn at my side. Dinner had been a unique form of torture. Sweet hell. I wanted him.

I had chosen for us to eat at a Japanese hibachi grill. While the chef cooked at the grill in front of us, Finn was relaxed and teased me all evening long. I was discovering that once he was out of his uniform, so to speak, he let down his guard. I imagined this was the man he was when he wasn't being all professional. He had thankfully explained the history I knew of him from Ethan. I didn't want to accidentally say something that gave away I'd been nosy about him. We drank sake, and I forced myself to stay halfway sober. I was in bad enough shape as it was.

I was punch drunk on the fumes of my desire for Finn. Our chef offered to create tempura-fried ice cream, nudging me slightly out of my haze.

"Fried ice cream?" I repeated. The chef winked at me and nodded. Of course, I said yes.

I'd never eaten at this place, but I'd heard it was fun. Finn, in fact, had eaten here before. I learned he loved food and was an engaging companion—funny, sly, thoughtful and could easily compete with me for flirting. He was shameless and reminded me of Ethan who'd won Zoe's heart with his relentless teasing. He regaled me with a few amusing stories from his soccer playing days and seemed rather circumspect about the change in his circumstances.

The set up at the hibachi grill was such that it was impossible to eat alone. We were seated at a wide counter with chairs circling the grill in the center. Another couple joined us, crowding us into the corner slightly when an extra chair was added. Being crowded against Finn was quite fine with me. The closer he was, the better as far as I was concerned. I glanced over at him.

"I was hoping you'd be in uniform," I said.

He grinned. "Ah, so you were then?" he asked.

I nodded and brushed a loose lock of hair out of my eyes, tucking it behind my ear. "I love your uniform. I can't be the only woman who told you it's a good thing," I offered.

He grinned again. My belly, which was well trained by his mere existence at this point, executed a flip. Our waitress swung by, serving another two tiny cups of sake. I sipped the sweet liquor.

"Well, luv, I only wear my uniform when I'm working."

I nudged his knee with mine. "But why?"

He rolled his eyes and shook his head, sipping his sake. "It's technically a rule," he offered.

"What about the cuffs?" I asked.

His eyes darkened. We'd been flirting like this all night. It was so delicious, it felt almost like sex.

"There are rules about those too."

"Explain."

I gave him another nudge with my knee. I couldn't resist any opportunity to touch him, no matter how small.

"It's a simple rule. You can only use your city issued police gear, uniform included, for official purposes," he explained, each word enunciated.

His sexy British accent sent a hot shiver through me. I twirled a lock of hair around my finger and cocked my head to the side. "So if you had to arrest me...?"

He chuckled. "If I had to arrest you, I don't think you'd find the handcuffs too comfortable. Or perhaps you would." he said, finishing my sentence for me.

His words sent a wash of heat rolling through me. I cocked my head to the side. "I just might."

I took another sip of my sake, just as his palm slid onto my thigh. His touch was like a hot brand. Oh hell. I was in trouble. I needed to care about how quickly I was spiraling out of control. Maybe. But I didn't give a damn. I glanced up at him. His blue eyes had darkened to navy, heat banked in his gaze. My body was like a bell only he could ring. The force of his touch vibrated through me, every fiber of my being alive and ringing.

I shifted my legs slightly, my body restless in response to his touch. I'd been wet for hours at this point. This endless night of teasing and flirting was coiling me tighter and tighter inside. Just being near him was foreplay.

"Are you sure you want to wait for dessert?" he asked, leaning over, his voice a gruff whisper in my ear. Goose bumps ran down that side of my body. I managed to nod. Because this was too fun. As much as I wanted to get to the next step, I didn't want this to end yet. At that moment, the man in the couple who had just joined our group started chatting with us.

"So what do you recommend for dinner?" he asked.

I glanced over. "It's all good."

"Do you agree?" he then asked, his eyes flicking to Finn.

Finn took a swallow of his sake and nodded. "Everything is absolutely delectable," he said.

Just as his fingers hooked the edge of my skirt and slid between my thighs.

Oh. My. God. I was going melt on the spot. I felt the flush blooming over my skin. I had to force myself to try to pay attention to the man's continued questions. He chattered on, oblivious to my state, while his wife sat quietly beside him.

Meanwhile, the calloused surface of Finn's palm against the inside of my thigh was enough to make me come right there. My channel throbbed, and I knew the silk between my thighs was wet. Finn managed to casually chat, tolerating the questions from the man beside us far better than I was. All the while, his hand inched its way up in between my thighs. I almost cried out when he dragged his fingers over the wet silk there.

Only then did I sense he was as rattled as I was. His breath hissed, his dark eyes flicked to me, the look there so hot, it nearly singed me. Our fried ice cream arrived, and I absentmindedly nibbled on it before asking if we could take the rest home.

Finn glanced down at me. "Not a brilliant plan, luv."

Distracted and in a haze with his fingers teasing me, I looked up at him, not understanding what he meant. "Why not?"

"It will melt," he replied, his low voice sending another ripple of heat through me.

I glanced down at my plate before taking two quick bites to finish it off. "Okay, I'm done," I announced.

I wanted to leave, but I didn't want to leave. I didn't want him to stop touching me, but it wasn't a smart plan for me to climb on his lap, although I was seriously considering it.

I looked over to Finn, crooking my finger. He leaned down, so I could whisper in his ear.

"So would you have to arrest me if I climbed on your lap right now?"

I heard him swallow and was gratified to know he might, just might, be teetering on the edge of his control.

"I might," he murmured.

Chapter Seven

FINN

By a bloody miracle, I managed to remove my hands from that sweet, hot spot between Jana's thighs and escort her from the restaurant. Need was pounding so hard through my body, I almost forgot to pay our bill. Her elbow in my side directed me toward the reception desk as we were about to pass by. After I paid, I caught her hand in mine and walked quickly outside, making a beeline for my car. I was seriously considering throwing my emergency flasher light on my dash, so I could speed to wherever we were going. As I let her into my car, I caught a glimpse of purple silk between her thighs when she swung her legs inside. Oh fuck. I was bloody losing my mind.

I climbed in the car, adjusting my jeans. My zipper bit into my hard cock. Dinner had been a few hours of torture. It had begun to rain, the pavement glittering under the streetlights. I started the car and glanced to Jana.

"Your place or mine?" I asked.

She met my eyes in the dim lighting of the car. "Yours. I'd love to see where you live."

I simply nodded and began driving. Just when I thought

I'd gotten a firmer grip on the reins of my control, she reached across and placed her hand on my cock. My breath hissed through my teeth. "I'm driving, you know," I bit out.

She laughed. "It's only fair play. You nearly got us into all kinds of trouble back at the restaurant."

I flicked my eyes sideways, fighting the urge to grin. "So true."

I drove faster than I should through the wet streets of Seattle. Pulling in quickly in front my townhouse, I rounded the car to let Jana out. The rain had picked up on the way home. After I closed her door, I curled my hand around hers, and we dashed through the rain. Once we were inside, I glanced to her. She hadn't worn a jacket and now her blouse was damp. Fuck me. This did not help matters. The nearly sheer fabric was now damp over her bra. I could see her nipples through the layers of fabric.

I hung my jacket and kicked off my shoes. She followed suit, stepping out of her cowboy boots. Somehow the fact that she wore bright purple cotton socks paired with her leggings only made her more endearing. She was an odd combination of sexy as hell and quirky. Padding through my townhouse, her eyes scanned the area. She paused in front of the windows. The lights of Seattle glittered in the rainy night, while rain fell in a mist just beyond the awning over the windows.

"Oh wow! You have a lovely view," she commented.

Beyond the few city streets between my townhouse and the water's edge, Puget Sound was visible. The harbor lights reflected against the water in a blur. I walked to stand at her side, sliding my hands into my pockets.

"It's nice," I managed.

Her scent drifted up to me. I glanced down to her. "You smell like strawberries."

She canted her head to the side, her eyes meeting mine with that lopsided grin of hers unfurling. "I suppose I do. My lotion smells like strawberries. I love it."

Not smiling when Jana was smiling was proving to be an impossible task. I felt my own grin stretching. "That it does. So tell me, shall we have an after dinner coffee and call it a night?"

I knew what I wanted, and it most definitely wasn't an after dinner coffee. It was to strip her bare and finish tonight buried inside of her. Yet, I didn't know if that's what she wanted. I was feeling rushed inside, like a rock rolling down a mountainside, picking up speed as it went. The more time I spent with her, the harder it was to imagine myself stopping at any point.

She shook her head swiftly, her silver earrings swinging. "I don't want an after dinner coffee. I want you, Finn."

The reins of my control slipped through my fingers. I forced myself to look away for a moment, scrambling for purchase inside. She pushed me to the edge of my restraint. I looked back at her.

"I suppose that's good then," I finally managed.

"Why do you say that?" she asked.

I turned to face her, lifting a hand and brushing a damp purple lock of hair off of her forehead and winding it around my finger as I stepped closer. "Because I want you too," I said simply.

After a week of fantasizing about her, two days of naughty teasing texts from her and a dinner that had been nothing but hours of foreplay, I stepped closer again, slid my hand into her hair and fit my mouth over hers.

She sighed, her mouth opening instantly under mine. Perfect, fucking perfect. I swept my tongue into her mouth, my hand tangling roughly in her hair. She fit against me perfectly. Her breasts pressed against my chest when I slid my hand free of her hair and down her spine to palm her bottom and pull her tight against my cock. She moaned into our kiss.

I was gone inside. Fucking gone. I could have kissed her for days. She tasted sweet, the hint of the sake we shared mingling with mine. While I let my hands roam over her curves, she got busy unbuttoning my shirt. Her hair caught on one of my buttons, and she giggled as she drew away to untangle it. When her hands slid over my skin, it was like lightning. I dipped my head, dragging my tongue along her throat. Her skin was slightly cooled from the rain. I slid my hands around her waist and up her sides to cup her breasts under her blouse. I loved that it was loose, so I could move easily under the sheer fabric. Her bra was lace, her nipples pebbling under my touch. I dropped kisses into the valley between her breasts, finally catching the bow at the center of her blouse and untying it with my teeth.

"Finn," she murmured on a gasp.

I lifted my head. Her eyes opened, wild and dark. We stared at each other for a moment.

"I can hardly stand," she whispered roughly.

I felt a sense of grim satisfaction knowing she might just be as out-of-control as I felt. Bloody hell, I wanted her. This wasn't just sex, it was something else. Something wild, a pounding need, a driving force I couldn't hold back.

I slid my arm under her hips and lifted her against me. "Let's find a bed. That way you don't have to worry about standing."

She laughed softly as I walked swiftly through the living room and down the short hallway, shouldering through my bedroom door. The lights were on motion sensors and came on as we entered. I nudged the sensor with my elbow, dimming them slightly. I eased her down in front of the bed and set to stripping her clothes off. Her blouse fluttered through the air, drifting to the floor as she shimmied out of her skirt and her insanely sexy knit stockings. I shrugged out of my shirt. She barely managed to get my jeans unbuttoned.

Once I saw her in nothing but her white lace bra and her purple panties, I couldn't think anymore. I nearly flung her onto the bed. She tumbled into the pillows, her rich brown hair, streaked with purple and pink, lay in a tangle. I stretched out beside her and settled in to taste every inch of her.

"You weren't supposed to be this maddening," I murmured against her skin as my lips made their way into the valley between her breasts.

She gasped. "I don't know what you mean."

"You make me crazy," I muttered.

I laved her nipples with my tongue through the lace. Her fingers gripped my hair roughly, her hips rolling against me as I settled between her thighs. My cock was so hard, I could hardly bear it. I didn't want to rush this though. I needed *all* of her. If this was the only night I had with her, I needed to make it matter. Warning bells rang in my mind, loud and clanging, but I ignored them. When she arched into me with a cry as my teeth closed over her nipple, I flicked my thumb under the clasp between her breasts. She had generous curves, her nipples were taut and deep pink, a contrast to her fair skin. Freckles were scattered here and there.

I drew a nipple into my mouth, swirling my tongue around it, savoring the taste of her skin. She cried out, rocking against me. My cock throbbed, so swollen with need I ached from it. I drew back, mapping my way down her body with my lips. I dragged my fingers over the wet silk between her thighs. We'd been in a state of foreplay for hours at this point, and I was nearly out of my mind, lust lashing at me sharply. I roughly tugged at the thin strip of silk, yanking it down her thighs. She kicked it free, and I sank two fingers into her core.

Her hips bucked against me. With my fingers buried inside of her, I dipped my head, dragging my tongue across her clit, and she came in a noisy burst against my mouth. She yanked my hair restlessly. Lifting my head, I glanced up. Bloody hell, she was glorious. Her skin was damp with a sheen of passion.

Just as she was in every encounter I had with her, she was brash and demanding.

"Come here," she said roughly.

Happy to comply, I started to settle over her, but she nudged me with her knee. "Oh no you don't. Get those jeans off," she ordered.

I chuckled. "Bossy, are we?"

"Yes," she said quite clearly, nudging me again with her knee.

I stood, and she rose up on her elbows, hooking my jeans with a finger and yanking at them. I chuckled again. Bossy though she was, her efforts were not effective. I stepped back and strode around the corner of the bed, snatching a condom out of the drawer on my night table. Kicking my jeans and briefs free, I rolled the condom on swiftly, my eyes on her the whole time.

She rolled back with me as I stretched out over her, her legs curling around my hips. Lacing my fingers into hers, I held myself still for a moment. Need was pounding at me so hard and fast, I could barely restrain myself. I feared I might hurt her if I didn't take a moment to gather my control. I rocked my hips against her, feeling her slick heat calling to me.

"Oh for God's sake, don't make me wait," she gasped.

She reached between us, curling her palm around my cock. In one swift surge, I sank into her, letting out a low groan at the feel of her creamy clench throbbing around my cock.

Chapter Eight

JANA

Finn sank into me, and I almost came instantly. It didn't matter that he'd already sent me into one spinning, glorious climax. My need was a fiery, endless greedy force. I curled my legs around his hips and rocked into him. He was hard and thick inside of me, the stretch of his cock inside my core so delicious I could hardly bear it. He held still for a beat and then began to move. Only for a few seconds were his strokes measured and in control. Then, we were pounding into each other, our skin slapping. He couldn't drive deep enough or fast enough. I dragged my tongue along his neck, nipping at him and savoring the salty tang of his skin. His hands gripped mine tightly.

"Jana," he murmured, his voice a gruff whisper.

I looked up, and the dark heat in his eyes nearly sent me flying. Pressure gathered in my center again. With every stroke, pleasure spun through me, radiating outward. I felt caught in a wave rolling faster and faster. Suddenly it crested, and the intensity of my release hit me so hard, I saw stars. Ecstasy rocked through me, tossing me in its current as I heard myself calling his name. He let out a rough, guttural cry as he went taut, driving deep one last time before he collapsed against me. He immediately rolled us over so that I was on top of him. I fell against him in a bliss, boneless and sated.

———

I didn't remember falling asleep, but I woke during the night, warm and relaxed with Finn curled up behind me. I took a deep breath, letting it out in a slow sigh. The bedroom was dark, but the curtains were open, so the city lights filtered in from outside. I hadn't fallen asleep with a man in over a year. My disastrous accidental affair had ended over three years ago, and my attempts at dating since then had been sporadic and unsatisfying. I'd spent one night with a guy I tried to make things go somewhere with. But that one night was what had persuaded me to stop bothering. I felt restless and hadn't been able to relax. With Finn, it had been so easy to relax.

I remembered the reverberations of my climax echoing in my body. I had vague memories of him slowly untangling himself from me, leaving the bed and then returning. He'd tucked us under the covers where I burrowed up against him. His breathing was steady and even. I wanted to roll over and look at him, but I didn't want to disturb the moment.

I knew I could be silly and brash. It was just how I approached life. I'd wanted Finn and set out to have him, yet I hadn't expected this. The level of comfort I felt with him made me feel so vulnerable, I didn't know what to do with myself. That should've made me tense, but it didn't. Not right now. I took another deep breath, closed my eyes and fell back asleep with his strong, warm body curled up around me.

The following morning, I woke up alone. Sitting up, I looked around Finn's bedroom. His bed occupied the center of the room—a four-poster bed, a matching dresser and night tables of dark mahogany were the extent of furnishings. The window faced Puget Sound from an angle. I looked out into the slate gray, rainy morning, wondering what to do with myself. Hearing the shower running, I kicked the covers off and climbed out, padding through his bedroom into the bathroom. The water turned off just as I walked into the bathroom. He stepped out of the shower, reaching for the towel hanging on the wall.

I took the moment to thoroughly enjoy the sight of him. Sweet Jesus. Did I mention yet it should be illegal for a man to look like him? He was cut, every inch of him fit. He turned and saw me at that point. His eyes widened for a beat and then he smiled. God, with water running all over him, I just wanted to lick it all off for him. This man made me feel like a swoony idiot. I should've cared about practically melting at the sight of him, but I didn't.

"Good morning," I said.

His mouth curled up at the corner. "Morning luv," he said simply. "Shall I make us coffee?"

He dried himself quickly, gesturing towards the shower. "Feel free to take a shower."

I took him up on his offer, managing a brief yes to the coffee when he asked again. I was rather stunned at my reaction to him. After I showered and dressed, I walked down the short hallway into his living room. I hadn't really absorbed it last night. His townhouse was decorated simply with splashes of color in the scattered rugs on the hardwood flooring and a sage green couch and love seat with matching ottoman anchoring the room.

His eyes landed on my purple socks, and he grinned. "I like your socks."

I looked down and wiggled my toes. "My socks?"

He chuckled. "I like a lot more than your socks, but they're fun. How do you like your coffee?"

"Just a dash of cream please."

I strode over to the island between the kitchen and living room. It sat at a curved angle in the corner, behind which were the counters and the stove. He poured a cup of coffee, added a dash of cream and slid it across the counter to me. Hitching his foot on a stool, he sat down opposite me. He took a long swallow of his own coffee and then cocked his head to the side.

"I have to work today," he said.

I smiled before I took a sip of coffee. This was a man after my own heart. He even knew how to make coffee. "This is delicious," I said, lifting my mug.

He smiled slightly. "I like coffee."

"I figured you had to work, what with the uniform," I said, gesturing to him with a wink. "Can I do a ride along?"

He threw his head back with a laugh. "No, Jana. You can't do a ride along. Don't you have to work?"

"It's Saturday, so I don't have to go to the office. When do we get to have dinner again?" I asked.

He was quiet, something flickering in the back of his eyes, before he lifted a shoulder in a slow shrug.

"When would you like to have dinner again?"

I eyed him, taking a long swallow of my coffee. What I wanted to say was tonight, but I was a little worried about how crazy I was for him. Like stupid crazy. I thought perhaps I should force myself to wait.

"How about next weekend?"

He nodded smoothly, not missing a beat. "Next weekend it is."

Chapter Nine

FINN

I closed the door to the interview room behind me and walked down the bustling hallway into my office. I sank into my desk chair with a sigh. Just as I was about to turn on my computer and check my email, Eli stepped into my office.

"Hey man, what's up?" he asked.

I leaned back in my chair. "Hey mate. Not much. Dealing with a couple of interviews this morning. You?"

He slipped into the chair across my desk. "Had a long night. Couple of parties on campus and a few fights broke out. Nothing more annoying than dealing with a bunch of drunks when you're trying to clear things up."

I chuckled. "Drunks aren't the best witnesses."

Eli rolled his eyes. "I'd say not. I figure they'll be waking up soon, and we'll deal with the mess this morning." He angled his head to the side. "So I heard you're handling the assault investigation for Ray Sutton," he commented, referring to an arrest two nights prior. Ray Sutton was a candidate for Mayor of Seattle and in the midst of a close race.

"It's gonna be a bloody mess," I replied.

He chuckled and then sobered quickly. "What were the arresting charges?"

"Fourth degree assault. The two responding officers didn't even raise it up to domestic violence assault. It sounds much worse than misdemeanor DV charges if you ask me. She had a bruised jaw and marks on her neck."

Eli groaned and shook his head. "You're fucking kidding me."

"Mate, I wish I was. Now I'm stuck trying to figure out where to go from here. I have a meeting with the DA later today."

"Who's the attorney on the case?"

"Becca McNamara," I answered. Becca was one of a number of DA's we worked with on a regular basis.

He flashed a grin. "Good. She doesn't mind a fight."

"Most certainly not. Bloody relieved she's handling this."

Eli nodded. "You wanna grab some lunch?"

"Sure. I could use a break."

I pushed out of my chair, snagging my phone and glancing down to see a text from Jana.

When you said next weekend, what did you mean?

I paused in the hallway to reply, laughing to myself.

The weekend would be Friday and Saturday.

Sliding my phone back into my pocket, I walked beside Eli down the street, making our way to Pike's Place Market. This was one of my favorite places to grab lunch. The choices were varied, and everything was good. Eli made his way down to one of the Thai places, while I snagged something from a bakery and sandwich place. We met up again at a cluster of tables looking out over the water. My phone buzzed in my pocket.

Oh, does that mean we get to have dinner Friday and Saturday?

I couldn't help but grin. Jana followed her text with a picture of a cake in the shape of breasts. I laughed out loud, forgetting Eli was sitting across from me.

"What's so funny dude?" he asked.

I looked up and shrugged. "Silly text from a friend."

He accepted my answer at face value. I wasn't up for explaining and certainly didn't want to show him the cake breasts. Not that I would be embarrassed about it, but it would say more about what was going on with Jana than I wanted. I ignored her text for now and put my phone away. After we finished eating, we returned to the office, and I got to work reviewing the notes from the various interviews from the assault.

Eli was right. It was going to be messy. Ray Sutton was a candidate in the latest Seattle Mayoral election. He was a family values guy on paper and in the media. Privately, he appeared to be a full-blown violent asshole. He'd badly bruised his wife's jaw and left fingerprint bruises on her neck. The team on call had responded to an assault report from a neighbor. My guess was there probably wouldn't have even been a call if there hadn't been a witness. Ray Sutton was drunk and the door to their townhouse had been left open. A witness saw him haul off and punch her. When she fell to the floor, they witnessed him grab her around the neck.

According to the report, Sutton kicked the door shut with his foot at that point. His wife wasn't talking, although she'd received medical treatment and had apparently spoken with the domestic violence advocate at the hospital. Since then, Sutton's media team had shut her up quick. But, we had a witness, and I had Becca McNamara on the case. She didn't mind a court fight, and she didn't give a bloody damn about politics.

I tapped the speaker button on my phone and called her.

"Becca, how are you today?"

"If it's not my favorite British cop," she said by way of greeting. "I hear you're stuck with the Sutton case."

"Aye, I am. What are you thinking?"

"I'm not happy with the original charges," she replied swiftly.

"Don't blame you. I've already talked with the responding team. I don't have a good answer for you, other than they're young and didn't handle the pressure from Sutton's attorney well. He was on site before they were."

"I know, but it doesn't change the fact we have a good case. We don't need his wife as a witness. We have an eyewitness. Do you know if she's staying with him?"

"Think so."

"I was hoping you could talk with her," Becca said. "You're good with anxious witnesses. She might relax when she talks to you. Our case will be stronger if she's willing to testify. Right now, they're only allowing interviews with her attorney."

"Heard the same, but I'll give her a call and see if I can schedule something. Would you like to be there for it?" I asked.

"Tell me when, and I'll be there."

"Got it. I'll call you later."

The line went dead, and I finally started checking my email. My phone buzzed again. I pulled it out of my shirt pocket and saw another text from Jana. I had forgotten to reply to her last one that came when I was eating lunch with Eli.

Is this when you start ignoring me? ;) I just wanted to know if it was Friday or Saturday. Or both.

Oh and here's a not-naughty cake.

She'd sent a photo of a dolphin cake. Yet again, I laughed.

Let's say Friday and Saturday.

I might be half-crazy, but I knew I wanted to see her more than once. The week was dragging on as it was. I put my phone away again only to feel it vibrate immediately. I pulled it out to see a gif of a dancing turtle. Where the hell she got that I didn't know. She also included another angle of the penis cake. By the time she finished sending me all the penis cake photos, I figured I would've seen the concoction from every angle.

———

The following day, I had confirmed an interview with Lynne Sutton. I'd been surprised when she answered my call directly. I met with Becca McNamara beforehand. Becca strode into my office quickly. She was quite pregnant. I grinned when I saw her, if only because the last time I'd seen her, she'd complained vociferously about trying to dress for work while pregnant.

"Hello Becca, how are you today?" I asked as she closed my office door behind her.

Becca patted her belly. "I'm fine. I'm only six months pregnant, and I'm ready to be done with this."

I chuckled. "Oh and how does Aidan feel about that?" I asked, referring to her husband.

She grinned. "He thinks I'm working too hard. For that reason alone, he'll probably be glad when this is over too. We're both excited about the baby, but he's driving me crazy worrying all the time."

I knew Aidan in passing. He was an ex-Navy SEAL who ran his own private security company here in Seattle. Becca was brilliant in the courtroom and lovely with her dark hair and blue eyes. I found it refreshing that she was aggressive in the courtroom, but nice in person. My experiences with other attorneys weren't quite like that. Often those who were aggressive in the courtroom were assholes outside of it.

Becca sat down across from me. "So how do you think this will go?" she asked.

I took a swallow of my now cold coffee and shrugged. "I never know. I think what we have to lean on is the fact we have a witness. I don't know how much pressure Lynne Sutton is under. With the bruising on her neck alone, there should've been felony charges."

Becca nodded emphatically. "Exactly. I couldn't believe the report when I saw it. Did you talk to the team that responded? They're not doing us any favors with lame, low grade charges when he bruised her jaw and strangled her."

"I spoke with them. I think they felt pressured not to file felony charges on a politician, especially one who's in the public eye right now. We'll see what we can do going forward."

Becca nodded. "Well, do your magic with this interview. We'll see where we're at after you talk with her."

We left my office, walking down the hallway together to the interview rooms. Becca went to wait in the observation areas while I went to get Lynne Sutton.

Moments later, I looked across the table at Lynne. She had a fragile quality to her with her small build and wispy blonde hair. The bruising on her jaw and neck was still visible. I took a deep breath and tried to focus. A maddening quality to interviews with domestic violence victims was they could be remarkably steadfast, either in their defense of the person who hurt them, or in their unwillingness to make things worse for that person by telling the truth about what happened. The sad truth was they were safer, statistically speaking, if they stayed with their abuser. I hated that. Victims were at greater risk when they attempted to leave their abusers with over 72% of all murder-suicides involving an intimate partner who left their abuser, and women comprising over 94% of those homicide victims. It was depressing as hell if I allowed myself to dwell on it.

Throw in the fact Lynne Sutton was married to an up and coming politician with a reputation to protect, and the odds were stacked against us we'd get her to talk. I was surprised when I asked a few questions, trying to start off lightly, and then she leaned back in her chair and sighed.

"Can I just say something?" she asked.

"Please do," I replied.

Her hands were shaking slightly and had been ever since

she sat down at the table. I presumed she was under an enormous amount of pressure.

"He did exactly what the witness said he did," she said simply. "I'm not returning home when I leave here. I'm going to stay with my family. It's the only place I can go where I hope he won't come after me. If you need me to testify, I will. I was hoping I wouldn't have to because we had a witness."

I quickly explained. "If you aren't willing to testify, I understand. We can go forward without it, but your supporting testimony will help the case since you're the actual victim. I'll be honest, it's rare we have a witness in a situation like this. More often than not, we might get a call because a neighbor hears arguing, but we can't press charges without the victim's cooperation. In this case because we have an eyewitness, we charged your husband anyway. The DA was hoping you might be willing to give us a statement as well."

Lynne sighed and nodded. "This whole thing just makes me tired. I was so relieved when you called me in for the interview because I've hardly been able to leave the house since the night he was arrested. I expected them to hold him that night. If I'd known he was going to be offered bail, I would've left, but then he came home," she explained, twisting her hands together and pausing to take a breath.

I bit back the urge to swear mightily. Bloody fucking hell. She didn't want to be there and hadn't since the first night. Because two greenies were too chicken to file the charges they needed, Ray Sutton had posted bail that same night. It had been a full three days since the assault, and she'd probably been living in terror the whole time. I had enough sense to know that this particular assault was unlikely the first.

I looked across at her, gathering myself. "Of course. I understand. My apologies he was released that night. If we'd been aware of the situation, it wouldn't have happened."

She swallowed audibly, and it was obvious she was

fighting tears. Stepping out of my chair, I went to a small table in the corner and pulled a box of tissues out of the drawer. Returning to the table, I slid them across to her as I sat down. She started crying, while I sat quietly with her. It wasn't that I didn't want to comfort her, but I sensed she needed a moment to cry.

After a few minutes, I asked, "Do you need anything?"

She lifted her head, blowing her nose noisily before replying. "No, I'm okay. Can you give me some suggestions on how to handle any calls from him?" she asked.

"Absolutely. We can have the DA file updated charges that include no contact with you. That way, you won't have to worry about calls from him. That will be part of the suspended court orders, assuming we get what we request. I can assure you the prosecutor assigned to the case won't buckle to public pressure. I suggest you remain here at the station until we handle this today. Will that be okay with you?"

She nodded quickly. "Of course. Where should I wait?"

"This room is fine. We don't need it right now, and it would be best for you to stay out of the public waiting areas. I presume he'll expect you to be home by a certain time, am I correct?"

Her *yes* was barely a whisper.

"We'll do everything we can to keep you safe. Can I get you anything while you wait?"

Once she shook her head, I stood, pausing beside her chair as I walked past it.

"Thank you for being honest about what happened. I know it's not easy. I can arrange for a DV advocate to come wait with you if you'd like."

She reached out, gripping my hand. "No, that's okay. I have a friend who will come sit with me. Thank you. I was worried I would tell you what happened and you'd tell me I was being ridiculous and I should've said something that night. I just..."

Her words ran out, and she simply squeezed my hand again before releasing it.

"You didn't need to worry, but I understand why you would. I'll go speak with the DA now, and one of us will come back to check in with you. Let me give you my number. I'm in and out of the building, so if you need something, call me directly, okay?"

She nodded. Though she was still teary, her shaking had stopped. "I don't suppose you have some coffee."

"I'll make sure we get some brought into you. Give me your number, and I'll text you mine."

Once she did, I zapped my contact over to her and then left immediately, circling around to find Becca and nearly colliding with her in the hallway.

"That was bullshit! There's a reason those guys should've filed more serious charges to begin with. If he hadn't had light charges, he'd never have been able to post bail the same night," she said, her eyes fairly snapping.

"Bloody right. I've already spoken with them, and I'll do so again. Next time, I'll make sure they clear any charges with the sergeant on duty, so we don't end up in this mess again. The least we could've done was make sure he was held without bail until a court hearing the following day. Did you need anything from me or did you get what you needed for the hearing from our interview?"

"I'm all set. I'm heading to the courthouse now to file updated charges and include a no contact order. Good call to have her wait here. I'll ask for an emergency hearing today and keep you updated."

"Got it. Call me if you need anything from us."

Becca dashed off. I was restless after this. I took care of some paperwork, and then headed outside for some fresh air and to grab a bite to eat. By pure habit, I hopped in my police cruiser and headed over to Desert Isle Coffee. I didn't need coffee in particular, but they had excellent sandwiches. A steady drizzle was falling as I strode quickly down the side street where I parked, shouldering through the door, the bell jingling above me as I entered. I was standing in line when I noticed Jana was there. She was seated at a corner table with her laptop in front of her. A man wearing a suit and carrying a look of entitlement was standing beside the table talking to her.

Jana looked uncomfortable. In every encounter I'd had with her, including when I saw her arguing with the guy who ran into the back of her car, she never seemed uncomfortable. Just now, she looked tense. The man reached over to touch her shoulder, and she flinched, angling away from him. Without thinking, I walked over swiftly. I couldn't say I had a bloody clue what was happening, but that didn't stop me.

"Hello luv," I said as soon as I reached her, sliding a hand onto her shoulder and dropping a kiss on her cheek.

I didn't even bother to be polite, stepping right to her side and forcing the man nearby to move. Her eyes whipped up to mine, slightly startled at first, but then a look of relief flashed across her face.

"Hi!" she said, a tad too brightly.

"Sorry I'm late," I added, figuring it was best if we went with the idea she'd been expecting me.

Her eyes flicked to mine and then to the man who was now off to my side. She got with the program right away. "Oh no problem. I'll finish up what I'm doing before you get your lunch," she said.

I glanced to the man beside us. I would imagine most women would say he was handsome. He had dark hair, dark eyes, and was impeccably dressed. He was tall with a slick vibe. He instantly annoyed the shit out of me. I didn't know who he was to Jana, but she didn't seem to want him near her. He looked my way, as if sizing me up.

"Well, I see you've moved on," he commented to Jana.

Her shoulder tightened under my hand. "Rick, just leave it alone. Have a good afternoon."

Rick, perfect name for him. Asshole Rick stared at her

for a beat too long, his eyes measuring her. I saw his gaze drop down to her generous breasts, which were showcased in her fitted, bright blue blouse. Tension coiled inside of me. A wave of possessiveness rolled through me, which didn't make a bloody lick of sense.

Rick simply nodded and then turned on his heel and walked away. Once he was out of earshot, Jana looked up at me again, her eyes worried. "Thank you."

"You okay?" I asked.

"Now that you're here, I'm fine," she replied, the cheeriness in her tone sounding slightly forced.

She seemed out of sorts. That bothered me. By nature, she was a lighthearted, bubbly person. I didn't know who Rick was to her, but I didn't like his effect on her.

"I suppose we should have lunch now," I added, watching as Rick went to get in line at the counter.

Jana still didn't seem quite herself, but she seemed pleased with this turn of events and threw a grin my way. "Perfect. Go ahead and take a seat. The manager is a friend of mine. She'll come take your order. You don't need to go wait in line with that idiot."

"I don't mind," I commented.

She looked as if she was considering something, and then she finally nodded. "Okay, can you get me a refill?" she asked, lifting her mug.

When I reached to take it from her, our fingers brushed against each other, sending a jolt of electricity through me. Bloody hell. She made me crazy.

I returned to the counter, standing in line right behind Rick. As the line moved forward, he glanced back to me, arching a brow when he saw me. "So you're Jana's new boyfriend?"

I didn't respond and simply looked at him.

"She's a lovely girl."

"How do you know her?" I asked because that was the only thing I cared to know.

"She used to work for me. We had a rather banging affair if you know what I mean," he replied with a sly grin.

Anger jolted through me. Not with Jana, but with Rick and the way he spoke of her. I surmised he was the very boss who'd thrown her reputation to the wolves. I curled my fingers tightly around Jana's mug. "Well, it's bloody obvious why it ended," I offered finally.

Rick looked surprised by my answer, his mouth falling open slightly before he snapped it shut. "What the hell do you mean?"

"You're a cocky prick and an asshole to boot."

At that convenient moment, the person in front of Rick finished their order, and the waitress called out for who was next in line. Rick spun around and ordered his coffee, leaving without addressing me again.

I returned to the table with a sandwich for myself and coffees for both of us. Sitting down across from Jana, I ate my sandwich and sipped on my coffee while she finished up what she was working on. Her hair was down today. The pink streaks had faded, although the purple was still rich. Her eyes flashed up to me as she closed her laptop.

"Did Rick say something jerky to you?" she asked.

I shook my head. "Doesn't matter."

She shifted in her seat, looking uncertain.

"He's an asshole and not worth worrying about," I added.

Chapter Ten

JANA

I followed Finn out of the café, flipping my raincoat hood over my head as we stepped out into the drizzle. He glanced down at me. "Did you walk or drive?"

"Walked."

"Need a ride?" he asked, his tone ever polite in his clipped accent.

I nodded. He slid his hand through my elbow and guided me down the street. I wanted to hug him, which was odd, but his timing had been so perfect. I'd been out of sorts ever since I ran into Rick. He was such a jerk. I couldn't quite believe I'd ever thought he was hot. I could look back and see I'd been in a vulnerable place with everything going on with my mother's breast cancer, but it still felt awful. I felt ashamed for falling for him, and ashamed for having an affair when I didn't even know it was an affair. Generally, I just felt shitty about the whole thing.

Finn was so matter-of-fact and gracious. He didn't even know who Rick was, but his comment that Rick wasn't even worth worrying about had helped. It had been nice to just have coffee and a sandwich with Finn after that. He led me down a side street and into his police cruiser.

I flipped my hood back and brushed my damp hair away from my eyes. "Oh perfect. I love this car," I announced once he closed the door on his side. "I can't believe I get another ride in this. It's not even official business."

He chuckled. "Only because it's raining."

"Oh, so you'd give anybody a ride in the rain?"

He looked out the side window into the rain and then back at me, a sly grin on his face. "Probably not. You push my limits."

I was feeling restless and reckless. I liked Finn. A lot. There was plenty of lust in the equation, but it was more than that. Running into Rick made me feel small and vulnerable, and I wanted to erase that feeling. Conveniently, or so I thought, the small computer monitor that had been in between the seats wasn't there today.

I glanced out the windows. We were on a side street, and it was pouring. No one could really see us. I climbed over the seats and straddled Finn, moving fast before he could dissuade me. I settled down onto his lap, my knees on either side of his hips. I could feel his cock hard against me. His eyes whipped up to mine.

"Jana," he said, his tone low. "What are you doing?"

"I'm sitting on your lap," I explained with a grin, stating that quite obvious fact. For good measure, I rolled my hips against him. Oops. Bad plan. His hard cock rubbed against my clit. I was wearing a skirt again, as I almost always did. I was a skirt girl. Even in the chilly, early December weather, I wore skirts with knit stockings to ward off the chill.

"I love your uniform," I said, running my hands down his shoulders and tracing the embossed label on his shirt.

His eyes darkened. He held my hips still against him, his fingers curling tightly around them. "We can't do this."

This was the good Finn, not the one that I knew when

he was out of uniform. He sounded so proper, and I just wanted to ruffle him, to nudge him to be naughty with me.

"Oh, Finn. Let's just play around a little bit. Nobody can see."

His head fell back against the seat with a thud before he shook it slowly back and forth.

I ignored him. I traced my fingertip along his jaw, savoring the rough stubble prickling along my skin. I dipped my head and kissed him. If he meant to resist me, he didn't try very hard. He growled into my mouth, his hand coming up to tangle in my hair, gripping it tightly as he devoured my mouth. I had been the aggressor, but he took over right away, and I loved it.

My nipples were tight, my panties were wet, and this was delicious. We kissed and kissed and kissed, deep sweeps of his tongue tangling with mine, his teeth catching my bottom lip, kisses dusted down along my jaw and behind my ear. I shivered all over, rolling my hips over the hard, hot length of his shaft. We got so heated, I forgot where we were until I lifted my head to catch my breath.

The windows were fogged. No one could see a thing, and the rain drummed on the roof of the car. We were in our own cocoon. I reached between us and unbuttoned his shirt quickly, gratified to find he wasn't wearing an undershirt because I wanted to feel his skin. I made quick work of my own buttons. Again, if he meant to stop me, he didn't try very hard.

I cupped my breasts in my hands, rolling my nipples with my fingers. "I want you."

"Bloody hell, Jana. You're killing me. We can't..."

I cut him off. "Yes, we can. Come on."

He shook his head, keeping his hands at his sides, balled into fists. He might be trying to keep his hands to himself, but the feel of his cock against me told another story.

"Let's make a deal," he bit out. "I'll make you come, but we save the rest for later."

Considering that I wanted him—every hard, hot inch of him—inside me, I felt slightly let down, but I would take whatever he was offering.

The second I nodded, his mouth was on one of my nipples. He swirled his tongue around it. I cried out when his teeth scored it lightly, a sharp streak of pleasure chasing away the vulnerability inside of me. His hands slid up my thighs, past the tops of my thigh-high knit stockings, the cool air outside a balm to the heat between us. He reached between my legs, dragging his fingers over the wet silk and then shoving it out of the way. Then, his fingers were inside of me, driving deep.

I rolled into his touch as he fucked me slowly with his fingers. I was so close to the edge, I was unraveling inside.

"Jana," he murmured, my name a guttural growl.

I opened my eyes, gripping the door handle with one hand and the console in the other.

"Look at me," he commanded.

I watched his face as he finger fucked me to insanity. I finally came when he pressed his thumb over my clit. He steadied my hips as pleasure radiated through me in a forceful burst. I fell against him, my body echoing from the force of my climax. Before I came out of my haze, he was helping me put my clothes back together and buttoning his shirt. I slid into the passenger seat, temporarily sated, but knowing I wanted more. I rolled my head to the side.

"Are you sure?" I asked, referencing his insistence only he would make me come just now.

He cut me off. "Later."

"But you said we weren't having dinner until Friday."

"I didn't say that. You did," he countered.

"Oh."

"You can have Friday, you can have Saturday and you can have tonight if you want."

"Oh my."

I drained my coffee, glancing up as Eli rounded the corner into my office. He sank down in the chair across from me. "So I hear Becca got the charges she wanted," he said by way of greeting.

"Of course. Did you expect anything less from her?" I countered. Though I'd been confident, I was relieved Becca had gotten what she was after. After my brief interview with Lynne Sutton, I'd felt we'd let her down and needed to protect her. A no contact order wasn't much, but it would help.

Eli chuckled. "Usually I wouldn't, but this one's got a lot of pressure. How did the interview go with Sutton's wife?"

"Much better than I expected. We got everything we needed. Because she was willing to talk, we were able to increase the charges. She's waiting here with a family friend until her parents come get her."

"They have kids?" he asked.

I shook my head. "Not yet. I'm guessing that's helping make it easier for her to leave. Gonna be a media firestorm the next few days though."

"Oh, I'm sure it will be. Good work."

I shrugged. "I didn't really do anything. She came in ready to talk. I'm still pissed about the original charges, but we're moving on. Becca did the heavy lifting on this one. Anyway, what's up with you?"

"Stopped by to see if you wanted to grab a beer after work."

For a beat, I was tempted to say no, if only because I had impulsively made plans with Jana tonight. I was seriously second-guessing myself now. I'd lost my bloody mind earlier. I didn't do things like what I had just done with Jana. Oh, don't get me wrong, I had plenty of casual sex. That was all I'd had since Kristen and I had broken up. But I didn't get hot and heavy in my cruiser with anyone. Ever. I was thinking it would be wise if I kept some distance between us, so I met Eli's gaze and nodded. "Sure. Tell me where and when."

"Harry's?" he asked in return.

Harry's was a pub nearby, a place we often frequented, if anything because of its proximity to the police station. Harry's also had good beer and good pub fare.

"Meet you there. Say 6 o'clock?"

He nodded and stood from his chair, exiting my office with a wave. I made a rather pointless attempt to focus for the remainder of the day. It had taken an enormous amount of discipline not to bury myself inside of Jana this afternoon. It wasn't just that she was sexy as hell. Oh, that didn't bloody help matters, but it was more than that. She felt vulnerable after lunch. The softness to her had hooked on a thread in my heart, unraveling it.

I'd stitched it up tight after everything that happened with Kristen. I hadn't considered that anybody could get to me like that again. Yet Jana had—so easily and with so little effort, it was slightly terrifying.

————

Late that evening, I leaned back into my chair at Harry's, taking a drag of my beer and chuckling at Eli's latest comment. There was an American football game on the telly behind the bar, and Eli was a fan of the Seattle Seahawks. For the most part, he was a rational man, but like most anybody who had a sport they loved, he wasn't rational when it came to this.

"I can't fucking believe that interception turned the whole game around," he commented, glancing to the screen and shaking his head in disgust. His eyes flicked back to me. "Oh well. I think this one's a loss."

"So where are you staying now that you and Beth broke up?" I asked.

Eli let out a sigh. "Crashing at my brother's place for a few weeks until I find a new one. I love my brother, but damn, babies don't sleep well."

I flashed a grin. "So rumor has it."

Eli's brother was also a friend of mine. He got married about a year ago and now had a newborn baby. "I'm sure you'll find a place soon enough."

"Oh, I could find a place now. It's just everything's so damn expensive."

"Bloody right," I added.

"Seattle's housing market sucks," he muttered with a roll of his eyes. "Anyway, let me know if you hear of anything."

"You looking to buy or rent?"

"Probably rent, but if I could find the right place, I would buy."

"You might want to talk to the realtor I used when I bought my townhouse a while back. She handles rentals and sales."

"Perfect. Give me her name," Eli replied.

I pulled out my phone to look up her number, reciting it quickly while he punched it into his phone. Our waitress swung by the table, picking up our plates and serving another round of beers. My eyes caught on my screen where

Jana's last text flashed. I'd sent her a text earlier to cancel. She replied with a sad face and a picture of a sad looking puppy. I wondered what she was doing instead.

I didn't have to wonder long because the door to the pub opened, and Liam Reed came walking through with his wife, along with Ethan Walsh and his wife Zoe. Lo and behold, Jana was with them. Bloody hell.

I knew Liam and Ethan in passing from my days as a footballer during university. They were Seattle Stars players, and our paths crossed back in university before I got injured. They were both good blokes, and I was glad to see they had done well for themselves. What I didn't know was why Jana was with them. She appeared to be friends with Zoe Walsh who I knew in passing from her work as a criminal defense attorney. Her relationship with Ethan had been a mini scandal at first because she had once been his attorney.

Jana's hair was damp from the rain, and she looked bloody gorgeous. From all the way across the room before she'd even seen me, my body tightened. I watched as she laughed at something Zoe said and then brushed a damp lock of hair off of her forehead, tucking it behind her ear. I wanted to walk over and kiss her.

Liam threaded through the tables. Considering that he hadn't even noticed me yet and could have no clue about what had passed between Jana and me, it was pure coincidence he commandeered the table directly beside the one I was sharing with Eli. Jana had yet to see me, and I wasn't sure whether I wanted her to see me or not. I had no good reason for canceling dinner with her, yet at least I was with a friend. Next thing I knew, Ethan glanced my way with a slight grin.

"Eh, mate. Long time no see," he said by way of greeting.

"Good to see you. How are things?" I asked as Liam pulled out a chair for his wife, a well-known orthopedic surgeon around Seattle.

Zoe sat down beside Ethan. Both Ethan and Liam were

smitten with their respective wives, and it was rather amusing. They knew me back when I was engaged, at a time
when both of them we're busy playing the field and rather
amused that anybody would settle down young.

"Right as rain," Liam offered as he sat down. "You?"

I lifted a shoulder in a shrug. "Fine."

I couldn't say I didn't still experience a pang when I
thought about my truncated football career. My car accident
and host of injuries couldn't have come at a worse time. If
my recovery hadn't taken so long, my window to return to
play would've been shorter. It was what it was, and I had
largely accepted it, but it didn't mean I didn't have some
regret. I was blessed in the sense that money wasn't a
problem for me.

Ethan glanced my way once they were seated. "I knew
you were still in Seattle, but I haven't seen you in a while."

"It's usually a good thing when people don't see me," I
offered.

Liam chuckled. "So true. Have you met Olivia?" he
asked, gesturing to his wife.

"Can't say I've had the pleasure."

Liam winked. "Oh, and it's definitely a pleasure."

She nudged him with her elbow. "Nice to meet you. I'm
Olivia. You are?"

"Finn Connors. I know these lads from back in our
university days."

Olivia was quite lovely with her dark curly hair, bright
green eyes and fair skin. She appeared to be a good counterpoint to Liam who'd been quite the tease when I knew him
before.

Jana waved at me as she sat down beside Zoe. If she had
a reaction to the fact that I canceled on her tonight, it didn't
show.

Olivia looked her way. "How do you know Finn?" she
asked.

"Oh, he was the police officer who responded to my fender bender last week," she offered in explanation.

Zoe flicked a glance toward Jana and back to me, her gaze assessing. "Finn is the nice cop who gave her a ride to work afterwards."

I inclined my head in a nod. "I certainly did. She had a flat tire."

"Is your car okay?" Olivia piped up.

"It's fine. The repair shop fixed my bumper and the tire rim that same day. It's good as new," Jana said, her eyes bouncing to me, a flash of heat in them.

I watched Jana, my body frustrated I wasn't closer to her right now. I introduced Eli to them, and conversation carried on. Somewhere along the way, Eli got up to leave.

"Can't be too late, or it messes up the baby's bedtime. Plus the Seahawks are losing," he offered with a laugh.

He headed out into the rainy night. Jana had gotten up to go to the restroom, and when she returned, her eyes landed on Eli's empty chair. She slipped into it, announcing, "I don't want you sitting alone over here."

Her sly gaze met mine, and my cock twitched. I couldn't help but grin in return. Her smiles were irresistible. She seemed rather pleased with herself. My effort to give myself a little breathing room from her was appearing rather futile. I was plain relieved she had stopped here for dinner and drinks with her friends, if only by chance. Because it meant that I got to be near her again. My body craved her. Lust was lashing at me lightly, the bite of it sharp and distinct. The scent of her drifted my way. Strawberries. I almost laughed aloud. Of all the things I thought could become a permanent reminder of someone, strawberries hadn't been on that list. My encounters with Jana had seared the scent into my brain, forever associating it with her.

Liam and Ethan were chatting about something. Zoe glanced over to Jana and me, smiling politely. "I don't know if you recall we've met a few times."

"Of course I do. We're usually on opposite sides in the court room."

Zoe nodded and flashed a wide smile. "I suppose we are."

Jana glanced between us. "Oh, I didn't even think about that. I bet you hate Zoe," she declared.

I chuckled. "She's just doing her job and happens to do it quite well."

I thought silently to myself that I hoped Zoe wasn't assigned to the newest case I'd inherited because she was a bloody good defense attorney. I figured that was best left unsaid. Zoe responded to something Olivia said, and Jana glanced to me. I could lose myself in her eyes—sky blue and impish.

"So I lost out to a friend for dinner?" she asked.

I thought about lying and saying I had forgotten I had plans with Eli, but it didn't feel right.

"I suppose so. I wasn't expecting this," I said, those last words slipping out unbidden.

Her eyes widened slightly and for a moment I thought she meant to tease. But she didn't. "Me either," she finally said, her words soft.

"So Friday then?" she asked.

Her question had the unintended effect of making me wish I wasn't so cynical about relationships. The way things played out with Kristen had hit me hard, if only because it had surprised me and came at a time in my life when I was facing major changes. I hadn't ever expected to want more with someone again.

I stared at Jana, the wheels in my mind spinning. I knew what my body wanted. I didn't want to wait to see her again. In reflex to how much I wanted her, I inanely decided to make myself wait and nodded.

Her mouth unfurled in a slightly lopsided grin, and it was like a kick to my heart. "Not tonight?" she asked, her voice lilting at the end.

I wanted to reach for her, tug her into my lap and finish

what we started earlier. But that wasn't a good idea. So, I shook my head, draining my beer and standing to leave.

"I have an early morning tomorrow."

Her smile didn't waver, but I saw a hint of the vulnerability I'd seen in her eyes earlier and it caught at the threads unraveling around my heart. I waved my goodbyes and left, falling asleep later thinking about the feel of her slick channel clenching around my fingers and that look of vulnerability in her eyes.

Chapter Twelve

JANA

I bit back the urge to swear, satisfying myself with a sharp glare at the phone on my desk.

"Of course, Mr. Simmons. Ms. Walsh will be happy to reschedule her meeting with you," I said so sweetly, my tone even annoyed me.

The demanding Mr. Simmons settled on a time, and I hung up, rather pleased with myself for not telling him to fuck off.

Zoe stepped out of her office and leaned her hips against my desk. "What's that look for?" she asked.

"Oh, that was Mr. Simmons. He rescheduled. Again," I said sweetly with a roll of my eyes.

"Oh God. He's such a pain in the ass about scheduling. I don't think I've ever scheduled a meeting with him that wasn't rescheduled at least three times," she replied with a slow shake of her head.

"Yeah, so I got to deal with him after dealing with my insurance company over that stupid fender bender. The guy who ran into me is being an ass. Even though they have the police report citing him as at fault for the accident, they're trying to negotiate a settlement and reduce the coverage. It's not much, but stuff like this just pisses me off."

Zoe threw a wry smile my way. "Insurance is probably more of a pain in the ass than Mr. Simmons. Let your insurance company deal with it. Don't take it on yourself."

She knew I had a tendency to get needlessly argumentative over minor stuff like this. "You'll be pleased to know I already told them to just handle it."

What I didn't add was I'd been irritable ever since I woke up this morning. I couldn't shake how out of sorts I'd felt since running into Rick. I'd managed to temporarily shove away my internal restlessness with that heated encounter with Finn. Yet, I'd been hurt when he canceled dinner with me. I shouldn't have been hurt. We had one date. That was it. I shouldn't be reading too much into it. But I couldn't seem to talk myself out of it.

During my restless sleep—the perfect time to ruminate needlessly—I'd convinced myself it was because of how vulnerable I felt after seeing Rick. Finn somehow made me feel as if I could let down my guard. That was *not* smart. The last thing I needed was to take something too seriously, too soon. I knew better. Much, much better.

"What's up?" Zoe asked, her perceptive gaze coasting over my face.

Zoe knew me very well, and she was my closest friend. If I could talk to anybody, it would be her. I leaned back in my chair with a sigh, twirling a lock of hair around my finger.

"I don't know. Finn and I went on a date last weekend," I blurted out.

Her eyes widened, and she slipped into the chair across from my desk. "How come you didn't tell me sooner? You hardly ever date. This is, I dunno, a *thing*."

I shifted in my chair, uncomfortable because it spoke volumes I hadn't said anything to her about it.

"I don't know. I think I really like him, and I think it's probably not smart."

Her gaze softened. "Why isn't it smart? He seems like a really nice guy. I mean, it's not like I've spent a ton of time with him, but he's a solid guy from everything I know," she said earnestly.

"I know. He's nice, but I don't think he does relationships. I mean, you heard what Ethan said. Ever since his ex dumped him, he doesn't really get serious with anyone."

Zoe cocked her head to the side. "You don't know that. Ethan also said he hasn't seen him much."

"I know, I know. That's just kinda how it feels," I finally said.

Finn was a flirt and a tease, and I'd read that the moment I met him even when he was being professional. That's why it felt okay flirting and teasing right back. I hadn't expected to feel the sense of vulnerability I did with him. Honestly, I hadn't looked for anything serious ever since my disastrous accidental affair. It wasn't that I didn't want to eventually find someone, it was more that a part of me felt like I didn't deserve it. It had been so hard not to take the stinging barbs about me seriously in the aftermath of that mess. Even though I could tell myself I'd been deceived, I still felt like an idiot.

I glanced over and realized Zoe was patiently waiting. "It's just a feeling," I finally explained.

She watched me for a long moment before leaning back in her chair and drumming her fingertips on the armrest. "Why don't you relax and have fun instead of worrying about more?"

"What makes you think I'm not?" I countered, feeling defensive.

Zoe eyed me, her gaze somber. "Um, because you just said so."

I stared at her for a beat and then bit my lip with a sigh. "I guess I did. I think maybe I'm being weird because I haven't had fun like this in a long time. Last time I did, it was a disaster."

Zoe sighed elaborately and glared at me. "Rick Douglas is a fucking asshole, and he lied to you and treated you like shit. That's why it was a disaster. Not because you read too much into it. You're a basically trusting person, and he took full advantage of that."

I restlessly twirled my hair around my finger as I looked at Zoe. "I know he was an asshole, but it didn't make it any better for me."

"Well, of course not. But it doesn't mean every guy is like him," Zoe explained.

"I *know* every guy's not like him. Ethan's awesome."

Zoe smiled slightly, her cheeks going pink. She'd never been particularly confident about herself in that way. I'd been so happy Ethan had seen right through her super-smart-professional-defense-attorney armor to the brilliant, beautiful, and sexy woman behind it. She was one of the kindest people I knew and hadn't hesitated to be there for me at a time when other friends—especially those I knew from law school—were more than happy to back away. Rick's law firm was prominent, and he had a lot of weight in legal circles in Seattle. Though his affair had dinged his reputation too, it wasn't anything like my experience. It was fair to say there was a double standard.

"I think Finn's a nice guy," Zoe repeated. "I asked Ethan about him again after we ran into him the other night."

"You did?"

"Of course. It's obvious you like him, and after I saw the way he looked at you, well, he definitely has a thing for you too."

"I thought Ethan said he hasn't seen him much lately."

"Well sure, but it's not like he doesn't have some background on the guy," she countered.

I was quiet, fighting the urge to ask her to spell out whatever she knew. I looked over at her and could see she was holding back a laugh.

"Oh stop it!"

Her laugh bubbled out. "I wanted to see how long you could hold out from asking me what Ethan said."

"Fine. Spill it," I said, circling my hand in the air.

"Okay, here's the deets. He's from London. Ethan didn't know him before college, but Finn completed his first year in university there before he got a full ride at University of Washington. Ethan says he's a nice guy. Finn's family is loaded apparently and pretty much nobody here knows that. Apparently, his ex fiancée didn't even know he has a trust fund coming his way when he turns 35."

My mouth dropped open. "You're kidding me. He's a cop."

"Exactly. It says a lot about him that he's not just sitting on his ass waiting for the money to come in."

"I guess so," I replied, wondering over that detail.

"Anyway, while Finn was in college, he got engaged and life was peachy as far as Ethan knows. Then, he got hit by a drunk driver and was badly injured. He broke a bunch of bones, and it took like a full year and a half before he was completely recovered and cleared to play. Ethan heard he had some problems with an infection with one of the breaks in his ankle. Who knows if he ever could've gotten back up to speed? By then, he had graduated from college and the world had moved on as far as considering him for pro play. He was all set to get married and just a few days before the wedding, she dumped him. Ethan says the rumor was she wasn't interested once he wasn't on track to be a pro player. Which sucks if you ask me. It doesn't matter to me at all whether Ethan plays pro soccer or not. That's not why you marry somebody," she said, her tone dripping with disgust.

I didn't even know the name of Finn's ex, but I promptly decided she was a heartless, shallow bitch. "What's her name?" I asked.

"Kristen. Ethan doesn't know much about her. All he knew was she was engaged to Finn once. He said she was pretty, kind of like a classic beauty—blonde hair, impeccably dressed and what not."

In short, nothing like me. I couldn't help but laugh. Classic was not a word anyone would use to describe me. If anything, I was the opposite of classic.

"Finn's probably just interested because I'm a novelty," I said.

"Oh my God!" Zoe slapped her hand on the armrest of her chair with an elaborate sigh. "You're not just a novelty. I saw the way he looks at you. Sure, he thinks you're hot, but you are. You're totally gorgeous. He likes you too though."

"How do you know he likes me?" I asked.

I felt like I was back in high school, swamped in uncertainty and all over a man.

"It's the way he looked at you. Wow, you are *really* into this guy," she said.

I shifted uncomfortably in my chair, picking up a pen and fiddling with it. "Why do you say that?"

"Because you're not usually like this over guys. It's more easy come, easy go. That's pretty much been the way it's been ever since you were with Rick. I know you felt bad about it, but you don't have to let it get to you like this. You haven't let yourself do anything other than be super casual," she offered.

I knew she had a point. It wasn't something I let myself think about much. "I felt like an idiot about Rick because I should've seen him for who he was."

"So what? Just because you didn't go into something assuming someone was a jerk doesn't make you an idiot."

Still flipping the pen back and forth, I shrugged. "I shouldn't have gotten involved with anyone at work. It wasn't particularly a great choice on my part."

"Join the club," she said with a roll of her eyes.

Zoe had gotten involved with Ethan when she was his attorney. "Not the same. Ethan adores you and he's an amazing guy," I said.

Zoe rolled her eyes. "Fine. I ended up with a great guy in large part because you pushed me to get over myself. I always look at you and think you're such a brave person compared to me. You're not afraid to put yourself out there, and that's what you did with Rick. Trusting someone is better than walking around looking at everyone with suspicion from the start."

"Yeah, right. Putting myself out there blew up in my face big time."

"I know, but at least you know who matters in your life now."

"That I do. You're my best friend," I said earnestly.

She cracked a smile. "Well then, why won't you listen to me?"

I wrinkled my nose. "Okay, what are you trying to tell me?"

"Relax and enjoy this."

"You hardly know Finn. What if he's secretly a jerk?" I countered.

Zoe glared at me. "I'm a criminal defense attorney. I have an excellent spidey-sense. I don't get the uh-oh feeling from Finn. He seems nice and down-to-earth. It won't hurt to try to relax and stop worrying over this. You've gone on one date. That's it. Don't make it more than it needs to be."

I stared at her, chewing on the inside of my cheek. "Fine. I'd pretty much talked myself into canceling dinner tonight."

"Don't do that!" she exclaimed. "I'm sitting here trying to sell you on this guy, and you don't even bother to mention you have a date with him tonight."

"I wasn't sure I was going," I muttered.

"Go. Don't be an idiot. Will it make you feel better if we double date?"

Part of me didn't want to do that because then I wouldn't have Finn all to myself. That should've been a bit of a cue for me that I was already in too deep. I trusted Zoe's judgment though.

"Yes, let's," I finally replied.

"Seriously? I thought for sure you were gonna say no."

I laughed and shrugged sheepishly. "Well, you totally got the scoop for me on him. The least I could do is let you come with us."

What I didn't say aloud was I might get a hold of myself if she and Ethan were there to take the edge off the madness I felt when I was around Finn.

In some ways, I was bold and put myself out there like Zoe said. Yet, it was a superficial thing. That's what had me so off kilter with Finn. Nothing felt superficial with him.

"Okay, when and where?" Zoe asked. "Oh and do you want to check with him about this first?"

"Nope. It's a double date. I've decided."

"You sure you don't want to check with him?"

"Yup. He can roll with it or not."

She laughed softly and stood from her chair, adjusting her skirt. As she turned and walked back to her office, I stood and jogged after her, catching her arm and pulling her around for a hug.

"You're the bestest best friend ever!" I exclaimed as I stepped back.

"Ditto," she said with a laugh.

I sobered. "No, seriously. Thank you. I know I'm a little nutty about Finn and not exactly rational."

"I get it. Totally. Don't forget how crazy I was with Ethan at first."

"Oh right. You took off for a few days while he was beside himself."

She nudged me with her elbow. "Exactly. You get to be nutty. Anyway, don't leave without telling me where we're meeting later. K?"

As she turned away, she glanced back once more. "By the way, you made a promise."

I *had* made Zoe a promise I would finish resubmitting my paperwork to finalize my legal courses. It had been a full three years since I'd had to drop out when my mother was sick. I only had another month left before the timeframe expired for me to simply re-enroll without re-applying. I needed to resubmit all the paperwork.

"I have three weeks left," I offered.

Zoe glared at me. "This is bullshit. You were one of the top students in our class. Don't get me wrong, you're an amazing paralegal, and I will feel lost without you, but you need to be an attorney. We've already agreed you'll join the practice with me, so do it!"

"How are we gonna find a good paralegal?" I countered.

"I don't know, but we will. Don't break your promise," she ordered as she spun around and returned to her office.

My chest tightened. Zoe was the best kind of friend. I almost started crying. She challenged me personally and professionally, and she had my back every step of the way. I only had a semester left of coursework to complete and then I had to clear the hurdle of passing the bar. Zoe would be there for this and be there to nudge me out of my comfort zone with Finn. Although I couldn't banish my worries over him, she might persuade me to try.

Chapter Thirteen

FINN

I stared at my phone and bit back another laugh. Jana's texts had become the highlight of my days, if only because they were so ridiculous. She'd texted me earlier to tell me our dinner date was now a double date with Ethan and Zoe, which was perfectly fine with me. Selfishly, I wanted her all to myself, but a dose of sanity might keep my body in check. It felt as if I were walking into a tunnel when it came to her. My focus was so narrow, I couldn't see beyond it. Not to mention, Ethan was a nice guy, and though Zoe was usually on the opposite side of me in the courtroom, I respected the hell out of her as an attorney. She didn't stoop to dirty tricks, and she was always straightforward.

After that text, Jana had sent a flurry of ridiculous pictures to me. Little did I know there was an entire industry dedicated to making naughty confections. I'd seen everything this afternoon, learning the penis cake on her phone was only the beginning. I'd seen breasts topped with elaborate icing concoctions, an entire human body mapped with icing, and a cock cake mounted bizarrely on the hood of a classic Ford Mustang. I shuddered to think of how the owner of the car had felt if they ever saw it.

I slid my phone into my pocket and headed home to change. No matter how many times Jana begged me to meet her for dinner in my uniform, I wasn't biting. I reasoned our impulsive encounter in my car was just a slip because I had actually been on duty and we'd had lunch together. But I couldn't go out of my way to wear my uniform just to please her. No matter how bloody tempting it was.

After a quick shower, I left to meet Jana. When I knocked on her door, she swung it open with a sound clattering in the background simultaneously. She spun away from the door. "Smokey! What the hell are you doing?" she called.

I looked over to see Smokey chasing a ball of yarn across the room, a broken vase, water and flowers scattered on the floor by the kitchen counter behind him. I bit back a laugh and watched as Jana walked across the room. I didn't mind the view in the slightest. She was wearing a skirt again, this one a little flirty number that twirled at the bottom. It hugged her hips and then flared out just above her knees. She wore a pair of black cowboy boots over leggings with a loose blouse atop her skirt. Her blouse was almost sheer purple silk, her black bra visible through it.

I doubted the effect she intended was for me to get hard upon sight of her. I swallowed and watched as she quickly picked up the yarn, snagged the dustpan, and started sweeping up the broken vase.

"Do you need some help?" I asked.

She glanced up with a grin. "Nope. All set."

After she dumped the broken glass in the trashcan in the corner of the kitchen, she rescued the flowers and gestured to a cabinet by the kitchen sink. "Could you grab a vase out of there and fill it with water? I think I can salvage these."

I stepped to the cabinet and found the vase she was

gesturing to. Turning, I asked, "You sure he won't just knock them over again?"

She shrugged. "Maybe, maybe not."

Smokey looked entirely unrepentant and sat on the back of the sofa cleaning his paws. I filled the blue glass vase with water and set it on the counter where Jana directed. I slid my hands in my pockets and watched while she arranged the flowers in the vase.

Smokey took that moment to do another flying jump into my arms. I caught him by a small miracle. "Bloody hell, Smokey," I said with a chuckle as I adjusted my hold on him.

Jana glanced at us and giggled. "Just be glad he likes you."

"Is he a test?" I asked.

She stopped what she was doing and stared at me. For a moment, her gaze sobered and something flashed in her eyes. The air between us hummed.

She gave her head a little shake and laughed softly. "No. Smokey's not a test. Don't get me wrong, I'm glad he likes you though. That's always a good sign, right?"

"I don't know if cats are as reliable as dogs about that," I offered.

"Probably not."

She rinsed and dried her hands quickly, before snagging her raincoat off the hook by the door. "Are we ready, or do you want to just stay here and hold Smokey?" she asked with a sly grin.

"We're ready," I said, depositing Smokey carefully on the back of the couch. He eyed me balefully and then set to grooming his paws again as I turned away.

In short order, we arrived at the restaurant where we were meeting Ethan and Zoe. The car ride alone with Jana had been a special form of torture. Strawberries. Again with the strawberries. I was the human equivalent of Pavlov's dog. I caught a whiff of Jana, and my entire body tightened in anticipation now.

She eschewed her hood as we dashed through the rainy

evening. She was laughing when we pushed through the door, brushing her damp hair out of her face. I glanced down and beat back the urge to kiss her. Her skin was damp from the rain, and her eyes bright. Bloody hell. She was dangerous for my sanity.

Jana glanced around, her eyes lighting up when she saw Ethan and Zoe in a back corner. She snagged my hand in hers and pulled me through the restaurant. She was a challenge to my manners. She didn't wait for anyone, or anything.

I allowed myself to be tugged along in her rather forceful wake, enjoying the swing of her luscious hips and the flare of her skirt as it twirled around her knees. My cock enjoyed it quite a bit as well. I forced my eyes up, reminding myself sternly that we were in a public place.

Ethan caught my eyes and flashed a grin as we reached the table. "Eh, mate. How is it?"

"Quite good. Yourself?"

"Good, good," he replied as we slipped into the booth across from them.

The waiter, decked out with a red and green bowtie to match the holiday decorations scattered through the restaurant, arrived to serve water for the table and then take our drink order. Zoe and Jana elected to share a bottle of wine, while Ethan and I ordered beers. The waiter reeled off some specials and then left. Zoe smiled over at me. I realized this was the first time I'd ever seen her with her hair down. In her professional world, she was a buttoned up lawyer—her hair always up, and always dressed tidily. Seeing her with Ethan, she was much more relaxed with a softer look to her. Bloody hell, he was smitten with her. He had his arm slung across her shoulders and chatted away, touching her in any small way he could as conversation continued. We got through the pleasantries.

Ethan asked how I was doing with work, and then there was the expected awkward moment, impossible to avoid when I ran into former fellow players. I'd known it was inevitable with him.

"So you've adjusted well then?" he asked.

I glanced over at him and shrugged. "Life's a roll of the dice as it is," I replied.

Ethan held my gaze for a beat. It had been close to a decade since that time of my life. While Ethan was still standing and playing along with a few others I'd known back then. Many others weren't. Injuries were fickle. I wouldn't say I didn't experience regret, but I had largely let it go. I hadn't had any choice in the matter.

Ethan nodded after a moment. "I was sorry to see how things played out," he finally said.

I shrugged again. "It was what it was. Things happen, and you either deal with them and move on, or you don't," I offered.

I felt Jana's gaze on me and glanced to her. If she thought anything of that brief conversation, I couldn't see it in her eyes. She shuttered them quickly and snagged her wine glass to take a sip. She glanced over to Zoe. "I don't think I told you that when Sergeant Finn here responded to my little car accident, and I let him look at my phone, I totally forgot about my screensaver."

Zoe's eyes took on a gleam, and she laughed softly. "Ah, so you must've had a good laugh," she said, looking my way.

"Oh yes," I replied with a chuckle.

Ethan looked between us. "What's so funny?"

"Remember Daisy's bachelorette party?"

"Yeah?" Ethan countered, circling his hand in the air.

"Well, Olivia had that crazy bakery cater it, and all the cakes were..."

Ethan finished for her. "Oh, those bloody cock cakes," he said with a shake of his head. He caught my eye, nudging his chin up. "This crew is crazy when they get together. Have you met Daisy? She's Tristan's wife."

"Can't say I have. I haven't seen him in a while," I explained.

I hadn't been particularly close to any of them, but we ran in the same circles just by virtue of what we did back when I was playing. Then, my accident happened. With a few of them here in Seattle while I tried to settle into my life, I saw them here and there. I'd encountered Liam a few times, and we grabbed a beer now and then. Same went for Ethan, as well as Tristan and another player from Britain, Alex. Yet, none of them had been a big part of my life after my accident.

I surmised it was due to their likely discomfort with the fact that I was no longer playing while they still were. It wasn't worth dwelling on, so I didn't.

"How is Tristan anyway?" I asked.

"He's downright domestic. The most committed bachelor I ever knew, and he fell for Daisy like a rock sinks to the bottom of the ocean," Ethan said with a wry grin.

I chuckled. Tristan had been a dedicated bachelor, not a flirt per se. In fact, he kept to himself for the most part. He made no waves and stayed out of the gossip circles. I'd been as surprised as anybody to find out he was getting married.

"Bloody right. He ribbed me a bit back when I was engaged."

Ethan rolled his eyes, sifting his fingers through Zoe's hair where his hand rested on her shoulder. He lifted a shoulder in a slow shrug.

"Aye. He ribbed me about you," he said, turning his gaze to Zoe and dropping a kiss on her cheek. He straightened and caught my eyes again. "Though he knocked some sense into me too. You couldn't talk me away now," he said it, glancing to Zoe again, the look in his eyes heated and unmistakable.

Zoe's cheeks flushed slightly, and she squeezed his hand where it rested on her shoulder before reaching for her wineglass. Glancing over to us, she took a sip of her wine and then cocked her head to the side. "So, I hear you're handling a messy case."

I knew exactly which case she was talking about. It had been splashed all over the news for the last few days.

"That I am."

"Which case?" Jana asked.

"The one the news won't shut up about. Ray Sutton got arrested for beating the crap out of his wife," Zoe said bluntly.

Jana looked to me, her eyes widening slightly. "That's yours?"

"It's not *mine*, but I'm the sergeant for the division handling it. My part is pretty much done."

"Mr. Family Values my ass," Jana said with a roll of her eyes.

"Bloody relieved you're not his defense attorney," I said when Zoe nodded along with Jana.

Zoe grinned. "I wouldn't have taken his case even if he asked."

"No?" I countered.

"Definitely not. I don't usually take cases like that. I'm not saying I rule them out completely, but I try to limit my clients to people I feel like I can legitimately defend. With good reason, Ray Sutton's not on that list. From everything I've seen about the case, you guys have a solid one."

"We do. For the moment," I added.

Zoe nodded with a sigh. We didn't discuss the case further. I was aware Zoe knew as well as I did that despite our witness and despite our currently cooperative victim, both of those factors could change. Our weakest link was Sutton's estranged wife until we got through the case. I'd even handled DV cases where we got all the way to trial, got through the conviction and later had the victim ask the DA if we could have the charges vacated. Usually bullied into making the request by her abuser.

Conversation moved on to lighter matters with Ethan

keeping up a steady stream of teasing. He clearly loved to ruffle Zoe's feathers. She was a more serious counterpoint to his lighthearted, playful personality. I glanced to Jana, considering how we might be perceived. When I was younger, I was as much of a tease as Ethan. Maybe not quite as shameless. I played my cards closer to my chest than him and kept things less public.

Yet, Jana was similar in that way. She had an edge to her —both teasing and bold. After seeing her interaction with her ex, I sensed that quality of hers was more superficial, almost a defense for her. My heart gave a hard thump. She was a flame I couldn't look away from.

Chapter Fourteen

JANA

I glanced sideways at Finn, willing my pulse to behave. I felt like a foolish girl around him. This double date idea was turning out to be a disaster, if only because it served to make me like him even more. He was a gracious and fun date. He and Ethan chatted about their early days of playing football back in London, regaling Zoe and me with a few amusing tales. I'd have expected him to perhaps be uncomfortable about the pro sports career he'd waved goodbye to after his car accident, but he seemed rather circumspect about the whole thing. When Zoe and I were chatting about a few work matters, he actually paid attention. He and Ethan teased about what it was like to adjust to life in the States, while he commiserated with Zoe about the backlog at the courthouse.

In short, he was a well-educated, gracious and amusing dinner companion. Oh, and sexy as hell. He also had his hand on my thigh for most of dinner, which sent my pulse through the roof, made my panties wet, and essentially made me crazy. I felt too vulnerable, and my body kept betraying me time and again. I was restless and uncomfortable with how much I felt. Needing a moment to escape from the sensory overload, I excused myself, threading through the tables to the ladies room. I was relieved to find no one was there.

After I went to the bathroom and washed my hands, I ran icy cold water over my wrists. I was so hot and bothered by Finn, I needed something to cool me off. I splashed water on my face and dabbed it dry with a towel, my eyes catching on the Christmas lights strung around the mirror. The holidays were when I missed my mother the most. I forced my thoughts off of her and pointlessly washed my hands again. The door swung open, and I glanced over to see Zoe walking in. She leaned her hips against the counter.

"Okay, what the hell is up with you?" she asked.

"What do you mean?" I countered.

I dried my hands off and tossed the paper towel in the trash. Reaching in my purse, I pulled out a tube of lip gloss.

"Don't you have to go to the bathroom or something?" I asked, casting my eyes sideways to Zoe.

She rolled her eyes. "Sure," she replied, pushing her hips off the counter and stepping into the stall.

"That doesn't mean I'm gonna stop talking to you," she called out.

I couldn't help but grin. When it came to women, a true friend was one who would carry on talking about important matters while she went to the bathroom. That was precisely what Zoe did.

"You seem stressed," she called out.

I unscrewed my lip gloss and swiped it across my lips, spending too much time getting it just so.

"Why do you say that?" I called in return.

The toilet flushed, and Zoe stepped out of the stall, coming to the counter to wash her hands. She caught my eyes in the mirror as I rolled the lip gloss across my lips once again.

"I said you look stressed because you look stressed. I

know you. Trying to make that lip gloss last a whole week?" she asked with a little laugh.

I sighed and leaned away from the mirror, closing up the tube and circling it in between my fingers. I turned away, leaning my hips against the counter beside her.

"I don't know. I guess I'm stressed because Finn's really nice."

Zoe turned the faucet off and gave her hands a shake, reaching for the paper towels. Drying her hands, she turned to lean her hips against the counter at my side and glanced over to me.

"Uh-huh. He's a nice guy," she replied. Looking at me quietly, her teasing gaze softened. "Why is that a problem?"

I shrugged. "Well, it's not. Except I really like him."

She tossed the balled up paper towel in the trash before looking back. "That's good. You actually like a nice guy. There's nothing wrong with that. Why don't you just relax?"

My throat tightened. I didn't know why Finn was having this effect on me. I hadn't thought much in a while about the shambles of my life after everything went wrong with Rick. In hindsight, I was more in lust than in love with him. Yet, I had liked him, and I'd had no idea what an asshole he was. I suppose the whole mess made me doubt my judgment more than I'd ever considered. My defense had been to keep things casual, and to have fun flirting because I was pretty good at it. Still spinning my tube of lip gloss in my fingers, I chewed the inside of my cheek and eyed Zoe.

"I don't know. What if he's secretly an asshole and he's good at hiding it?"

Zoe sighed. "I'm pretty sure he's not. It's just not the vibe I get from him at all," she said firmly, adding, "...and neither does Ethan."

I took a deep breath, letting it out slowly. "How much are you talking to Ethan about this? Because it's kind of embarrassing."

"Not a lot. He doesn't know you're all out of whack

about it. I just told him I thought Finn liked you, and I wanted to make sure he's a good guy. That's all."

I leaned my head back, staring at the ceiling. "Okay, okay. It's not a guy thing."

"I know. He thinks I'm being the overprotective friend. Which I am," she said with a little laugh. "This doesn't have to be any bigger than it is. You finally met a guy who's hot, you actually like him, and he actually likes you. That's it. That's all that's happening. You don't have to make it more than it is, but maybe try to relax."

I absorbed her words. What she said made perfect sense. I didn't need to make this more than it was, so why was I such a mess inside?

I caught her eyes, the understanding there grounding me and nudging me out of the mental circles I was running inside my mind. I laughed, taking another deep breath and letting it out slowly. "Fine. I'll try to relax."

She stepped closer to me and slipped her arm around my shoulders, giving me a squeeze. At that moment, a pair of women entered the restroom. They looked in our direction, one of them smiling as soon as she saw us.

"Girl talk?" she asked.

Zoe and I nodded in unison.

"Perfect. That's why we're here," she replied.

They laughed with us.

"Shall we share? Maybe group advice is better," the other woman said.

"Well, what's your problem of the evening?" I asked, happy to have the focus off of myself for a moment.

One of the two, a woman with curly blond hair and wide brown eyes, spoke, gesturing to her friend. "She just found out the guy she's been dating has a different definition of exclusive than she does."

The other woman with brown hair and blue eyes sighed. "Yeah, so he's an asshole, and I'm an idiot."

Zoe and I looked at each other and back to them.

"Better to find out now rather than later," I offered tentatively, my heart going out to her. Having had a variation on her experience, I knew how it felt to stumble into being the idiot. It sucked.

"Exactly what I said," the blonde haired woman said with a vigorous nod.

"What's your issue?" the brown haired woman asked.

Zoe thumbed in my direction. "Well, her last relationship was a fiasco because he definitely had a different definition of exclusive. I'm trying to tell her the guy she's with tonight is a really nice guy, and she should try to relax and give him a shot."

The women both looked at me. "Well, what do you have to go on?" one of them asked.

"My opinion, my husband's opinion and hers too. He's totally a decent guy. She's just freaked out," Zoe replied.

The women looked to me expectantly, the brown haired one speaking. "Even you think he's nice?"

I nodded. "Yes, I'm just..."

She cut in. "And you like him?"

"Yes, but..."

"Girl, don't be stupid. Unless you want to be alone, you gotta give someone a chance."

Moments later, we left the ladies room after I received my pep talk. When we returned to the table, Ethan glanced up, arching a brow. He looked to his watch and then back to us. "That was a bloody long bathroom break."

Zoe rolled her eyes and flashed a grin. "We ran into some friends," she offered.

Finn's eyes caught mine. The heat banked in his gaze nearly melted me and completely wiped out any efforts I'd made to cool the fire burning inside of me. When I sat down, I had to squeeze my thighs together to quell the sweet ache there.

He's a nice guy. Don't freak out about that.

Most of my struggle came from the discomfort of feeling

out-of-control. I hadn't felt this way since everything blew up with Rick. That event had collided with dealing with my mother's cancer and her death. The aftermath had left me feeling emotionally out of whack.

———

Finn pulled up in front of my house. Throughout the entire ride home, my body had been on fire. I was coming to realize I only had two choices: never see him again to somehow get control of myself, or give in to what I wanted because, sweet hell, I wanted him. Like mad.

Looking into his eyes, my heart was pounding wildly and my breath was shallow. I tried to think of what to say.

"Come in," were the only words that came out.

It wasn't a question, although it wasn't quite an order either. It was more of a breathy, ridiculous statement.

Finn simply nodded. In a flash, he was out of the car and opening my door, ever the gentleman. I swung my legs out and glanced up to realize his eyes were caught on where my skirt rode up on my thighs. The only relief I felt came from the recognition this attraction was definitely not one-sided. Thank God because it would be mortifying if it was. He reached for my hand, helping me up. That simple point of contact from his hand gripping mine sent heat licking through my veins.

I was galvanized, my body driven to get as close as possible to him. I curled my hand into his. I dimly heard the car door closing and then I was pulling him behind me, along the slate walkway and up the stairs to my place. We stumbled through the door.

Finn spun me around, my back slamming against the door. His lips collided with mine. Our kiss was like a flashpoint, the contact burning hot instantly. It was wet, messy, and needy, and I couldn't get enough. I yanked at his shirt. When I got the buttons undone, I ran my hands over his chest, savoring the feel of his skin, hot under my touch. He was hard everywhere, his body a work of muscled art.

He made quick work of my blouse, yanking it up over my head. Breaking our kiss with a muttered swear, his eyes flicked down on a ragged breath.

"Fuck me, Jana. I thought I was going to bloody lose my mind tonight," he said in a gruff murmur.

I gasped, rolling my hips against him. His cock was conveniently nestled, hot and hard, in the cradle of my hips, right where I wanted it.

"You thought you were gonna lose your mind? You're dangerous. I don't think I can be seen in public with you."

He chuckled, his lips making their way down my neck. His teeth nipped at the sensitive skin, the scrape of his stubble sending hot shivers through me. He rolled his thumb across my nipple through the black lace. I moaned, arching into his touch. I needed more. I needed everything all at once. I wanted it slow and fast, soft and hard. I tore his jeans open, sliding my hand into his briefs and shoving his jeans out of the way. His cock sprang free, and I curled my palm around it, sighing at the feel of the velvety, hot skin.

"Fuck, Jana," he groaned, lifting his head, his eyes catching mine.

We stared at each other for a moment, his thumb coasting across my nipple. My heart clenched. My need was a gathering storm inside of me, mingling with this intense feeling I didn't know what to do with. The only relief was to lose myself in sensation with Finn. I stroked along his cock just as he flicked his thumb between my breasts, undoing the clasp of my bra. I moaned in relief. My breasts were tight and achy, my nipples so taut, they hurt. I cried out when he dipped his head, his mouth closing over one of my nipples. His touch wasn't soft, it was rough and ragged, just how I felt inside. His teeth scored my nipple, drawing it sharply into his mouth.

I moaned his name with a husky cry. I gripped his hair

with one hand and his cock with the other, stroking him roughly as he set out to drive me near to madness, alternating between my breasts. His knee slid between my thighs, and I rolled my hips restlessly against him, chasing after the sweet, sharp pleasure streaking through me. I was so close to the edge when he suddenly lifted his head and stepped back.

His breath heaved, his eyes locked to mine, hot and dark. My body was a storm inside, of need and emotion lashing at me, whipping each other into a frenzy.

"I need to feel you," he said roughly.

Before I could even form a thought, he lifted me against him. I curled my legs reflexively around his hips, gasping at the feel of his cock rubbing against my pussy through the layers of fabric between us. My panties were drenched, and his cock slid against the damp silk as he carried me across the room.

"Bedroom?" he murmured gruffly, his eyes locked with mine.

I nudged my head toward a door behind us. Beyond the kitchen and living room, there were two doors—a bathroom and the bedroom. He followed my gesture and kicked the door open with his foot. I glanced down at Smokey, sound asleep on the couch, as we passed by. I was relieved he wasn't the friendliest cat at the moment. As we passed through the doorway, I reached out, flicking the single lamp on in the bedroom. Finn conveniently kicked the door shut behind him and walked straight to the bed. The lamp beside it cast the room in a soft glow.

He eased me onto the bed, and I was instantly disappointed, not because I didn't want to get naked. I was in a damn hurry to get naked, but any separation from him was a disappointment. I flung my bra to the floor, while he reached for my skirt and peeled it down my hips as I kicked my cowboy boots and leggings free, giggling when one of my boots bumped into him on the way to the floor. Greedy for him to be bare, I reached for him, tugging his jeans down roughly, giggling again when he got tangled and almost stumbled.

His jeans fell to the floor. He caught them in his hand and pulled a condom out of his wallet, tossing it onto the bed beside me. His dark eyes coasted over me, lighting fires on my skin everywhere they landed. The temporary pause gave me a chance to do what I'd wanted to do for hours. I leaned up on my elbows and dragged my tongue along the underside of his cock, gripping it in my hand and kissing the tip.

He groaned and started to say my name, but it was lost in another groan when I took him in my mouth. His cock was so hard and thick. I drew him in deeply, sliding back slowly and then down again, glancing up through my eyelashes. He tangled a hand in my hair, gripping it tightly, his eyes watching me. Curling my fist around him, I let it slide up and down in rhythm with my mouth as I settled in to drive him wild. Just when I thought I might be about to push him over the edge, he muttered something and then stepped back swiftly. He stretched out over me, roughly gripping my hands in his, lacing his fingers with mine and stretching my arms above my head.

His eyes locked with mine, the look in them so intense, my heart thumped in response. "Am I gonna have to cuff you?" he asked gruffly.

His words and the feel of his cock sliding against my wet pussy nearly made me come. "You might have to," I said with a giggle.

"Maybe next time," he murmured.

"Promises, promises."

He chuckled and then reached for the condom rolling it on quickly. He rocked his hips against me, his hard cock sliding through my folds and over my clit. The storm lashed inside of me. Another slow slide against me. My eyes closed with a sigh, the pleasure so intense I could hardly bear it. When I opened them, his gaze was waiting. My heart gave a hard kick, emotion tightening in my chest. To have this raw desire vibrating between us and feel this intimacy, I didn't know what to do with it. It was tangled up with my need for him.

I was restless and wanted to feel more in control. Rolling swiftly, I unseated him. Straddling him, I glanced down with a grin. "There. Right where I want you."

I thought for a moment he might try to take control again, but he didn't. His mouth curled up at the corner, one of those dangerous grins of his, and he gripped my hips, lifting me slightly. I reached between us, guiding his cock into my entrance. I sank down slowly, savoring the delicious stretch of him filling me.

Chapter Fifteen

FINN

Jana sat astride me, her creamy clench gripping my cock. She felt so good, tight and slick around my cock. Staring up at her, my breath caught and my heart thudded against my ribs. I didn't know what to do with the way she made me feel, but I couldn't look away. I gripped her hips tightly, watching vulnerability flash in her eyes. I felt a dash of relief. At the least, she felt perhaps similar to how I did.

She held still for a moment and then started to move, her hips rising and falling in a slow roll. She'd already brought me nearly to the edge with her wild mouth. I hung onto the thin thread of my restraint. She seemed to need to take control right now, so I let her. She set a steady pace, her channel pulsing around me. For several strokes, her rhythm was measured, but then we lost control together. My hips rose up to meet her, my back arching as she rode me. Her channel throbbed, slick and wet, around me. I reached between us, pressing my thumb against her clit.

My name came in a rough shout from her. Her sex clenched me tightly, sending my own release hurtling through me, the force of it so strong, my body went limp as

I spent myself inside of her. She collapsed against me, and I curled my arms around her. My hand tangled in her hair as we lay there, our breath heaving in the quiet bedroom. After a few moments, she lifted her head and raised herself up on an elbow. She traced circles on my chest as she looked down at me. One look at her flushed face, her lips swollen from our kisses, her hair a wild mess, and my cock twitched again.

She grinned that lopsided grin of hers. I shrugged, unabashed. I might not know what to think of any of what was happening with her, but I wasn't ashamed of the fact I wanted her like mad. There was no sense in hiding it. Still tracing circles on my chest, she looked at me quietly, her gaze sobering. My heart gave another hard thump.

She grinned again. "So, the cuffs?"

I chuckled, alternately amused and aroused at the idea of cuffing her to the bed and driving her wild. "I don't have them with me."

"Okay, but I have expectations."

"Fair enough," I replied.

"Shower?" she asked.

"Sounds good."

She slowly rose up, my cock sliding out of her. I instantly missed her closeness and feeling physically linked with her. That should've worried me, but I ignored it. Following her into the shower, I couldn't resist kissing her. She was bare naked with soap bubbles sliding over her delectable curves. Before I knew it, we were twined against each other again. I was sinking inside of her against the tile wall. It was only when I was buried deep that we realized together I didn't have a condom on.

I stared at her. "I don't..."

She shook her head sharply, cutting me off. "A little late for that now. We both forgot."

I didn't say it, but I couldn't fucking believe myself. I didn't forget things like this, but then Jana made me bloody lose my mind.

"Are you...?" My words trailed off when she cut me off again.

"On the pill. Yes, I am," she said firmly.

"I'm clean," I offered.

We held still, me buried deep in her core, our eyes locked for a moment, deciding together whether this was crazy or not. She suddenly nodded. "Sure you are. I trust you."

"Ditto."

She caught my lips in a kiss and then I pounded into her, hot water streaming over us, her channel clenching around my cock as I poured my release into her.

I bundled her into my arms later as we fell asleep.

Chapter Sixteen

JANA

"Why the hell are you here?" I asked Rick as I looked up from where I was working on my laptop.

I often came by Desert Isle Coffee after work if I had a few things to finish up. Rick had interrupted my time. Rick, his cockiness and arrogance once a turn on, only managed to grate on me now. He adjusted his overcoat and slipped into the chair across from me.

"I wanted to say hello," he said.

"Hello. There we said it. I don't want you to join me."

He stared at me. "Jana, come on. You know we had something great before."

I glared at him. "Rick, it wasn't something great. We had an affair that I didn't know was an affair. It was a huge mistake, and I never would have let anything happen if I'd known you were married."

"I'm not married anymore," he offered with a jaunty grin.

I rolled my eyes. "Yeah and you haven't been for two years. Whatever Rick, I'm not interested. Please leave me alone."

"Come on, Jana. You're not gonna find anything like what we had. We have chemistry," he said, arching a brow and winking.

My stomach actually turned, not the good kind of turn. I shook my head. "Rick, get over it. Please leave."

His grin faded. After a moment, he shook his head, looking more annoyed than anything else. "Fine, Jana. Good luck with your legal career," he said with a roll of his eyes.

"Fuck you," I said as he walked away.

We'd hardly spoken in the aftermath when our affair came out publicly. He quickly distanced himself and let me take the brunt of the public shame. He made me sick and what made me even sicker was that I'd ever had anything to do with him.

He ordered a coffee and left. My chest felt tight. I was anxious and out of sorts and had been for days. I hadn't been able to bring myself to pull it together after my night with Finn. We'd had another night the following night. I'd wanted him to stay Sunday night as well, but I forced myself to act like I had plans. I didn't, but it was too comfortable. I liked him too much, and I didn't know what the hell to do about it.

I knew Zoe would tell me to relax and stop worrying, but it felt like we were in this strange bubble, one neither one of us had expected to be in. I found myself fighting the urge to relax about it because I felt too comfortable with it and with him.

I sensed Zoe was right—Finn wasn't anything like Rick. Yet, I hadn't expected my heart to be at risk. Restless and missing Finn, I shook my worries away, slipped my phone out and tapped out a text.

So how was your Sunday and your Monday and your Tuesday? Obvious fact: today is Wednesday.

I pulled up a silly gif. I was all out of my naughty cake pics, so this time I sent a silly puppy photo, then put my phone away and tried to focus on work. All the while wondering if the heated spark that I felt with Finn would ever fade. Spark didn't accurately capture it, it was more like a bonfire.

Chapter Seventeen

FINN

I hung up the phone and leaned back in my chair, snagging my cup of coffee and taking a sip. It was cold. No surprise as my morning had been quite busy. Ray Sutton's lawyers were in a flurry, demanding records, arguing over petty details and filing a request to have the no contact order lifted. I'd been busy communicating with Lynne Sutton and her attorney about it, and coordinating with Becca. The aggressive stance taken by his legal team wasn't a surprise given Ray's current prominent role in the election and the family values image he was trying to project. I was hoping Becca would persuade his attorney that dragging the case through the public eye with more hearings wouldn't help his image. Time would tell.

I stood and headed to the break room to grab another cup of coffee. My phone buzzed, and I pulled it out of my pocket. I'd missed getting texts from Jana the last few days. Ever since the weekend, it had been radio silence from her. This should have been fine with me, but it wasn't. I sensed she was getting skittish, and I thought I knew why. Things were intense, far more intense, than I'd expected. Intense enough that I found myself shying away from thoughts about her. Two nights together, and I hadn't wanted to leave Sunday.

Instead of a text from Jana, it was a text from my ex. Fuck. Every so often, Kristen would text out of the blue. I couldn't say I knew why, but here she was again.

Hope this text finds you well. I was wondering if you'd like to grab coffee some time.

WTF? Staring down at my phone as I rounded the corner into the break room, I wasn't thinking when I spoke aloud to my phone. "No. I wouldn't like to have coffee sometime."

I heard a laugh and glanced up to see Eli sitting at the table. "You don't want to have coffee then?" he asked.

I flashed a slightly embarrassed grin, deleting Kristen's text without replying and stepping to the counter to pour a fresh cup of coffee. "I'll have coffee with you. Just talking to my phone."

"Who won't you have coffee with?" he asked slyly.

"Kristen. Every now and then, she texts me. No idea why."

Eli rolled his eyes. "Come on, dude. She's fishing."

"Fishing for what?" I countered as I slouched into the chair across from him.

"My guess is she's not hooked up with anybody else steady. Every time you hear from her out of the blue, she's in between guys. She's got serial monogamist stamped all over her," he explained.

"What the bloody hell is that?" I asked with a laugh.

"People who always commit. But when things aren't working out, they break up and then call all of their exes because they don't like to be out of a relationship."

"You've got to be fucking kidding me."

Eli shook his head slowly. "Nope. Not kidding. I don't know though, just throwing that out there. Maybe she just wants to have coffee."

I considered the timing of when Kristen had reached out to me in the past. "Eh, you're probably right."

After Kristen and I had first broken up, the ripples in our circle of friends had kept me a little more informed than the last few years. I hadn't gone digging, but I had known she tended to go from one committed relationship to the next. Now that I thought about it, she did tend to reach out in between guys.

"Bloody relieved I dodged a bullet with her," I offered.

My mind spun to the weekend with Jana. It was far more intense than anything I'd ever experienced with Kristen. We had been young when we first got together. I was a high-flying footballer with my eye on the pros. We were both in university, and sex was hot and heavy. I wouldn't go so far as to say I hadn't loved her. I had. It was just a different kind of love, less deep and less intimate. The second that thought passed through my mind, my heart thudded. Hard. I shifted quickly in my chair.

Eli looked over at me. I moved the topic to work, easy to talk about at the moment with Ray Sutton's case keeping the media busy. "How's your day been?"

"Eh, busy with paperwork today. Guessing you're tied up with Sutton's case. How's his ex holding up?"

"He's putting pressure on her with trying to get the no-contact order lifted. She's pretty stressed out about it. I think it'll hold, but it's a nuisance," I explained.

"It will. Sutton's gonna keep Becca on her toes though."

"That he will. She doesn't mind though, she loves the fight."

We chuckled, and then a few other people filtered into the break room. I stood to return to my office, pausing before I walked off. "Any luck finding a place yet?" I asked.

"Working on it. You didn't mention Shari was hot as hell," Eli replied, referring to the realtor I'd recommended to him.

I chuckled and rolled my eyes. "She's a professional. Treat her like one."

"Always," he countered with a wink.

"Well, when you find a place, let me know if you need help moving."

With a wave, I left, narrowly avoiding a collision with two women from human resources whose arms were filled with Christmas lights. They'd been decorating the station around everyone as we worked.

Returning to my office, my mind spun back to my conversation last week with Eli about his break up with Beth. I considered his explanation that he'd broken up with her, if anything, because it didn't make him all upset. Before Kristen dumped me right before our wedding, I would've said I wanted to settle down. After that, I got cynical about commitment.

Unlike Kristen, I wasn't a serial monogamist. She seemed to be on the hunt to find the magic man with whom she would want to settle down. I'd shrugged off that possibility. Or so I'd thought. Yet with Jana, for the first time, I wanted all kinds of things. I wanted more of how I felt when I was with her. The feeling between us was almost a stealth intimacy with its own power and force.

The following afternoon, lo and behold, Kristen showed up at my door when I'd just walked in from finishing an early shift.

"What the fuck?" was exactly what I said when I opened the door and saw her standing there.

Kristen ignored my greeting. "Finn! I decided to just stop by when I didn't hear back from you."

I stared at her, gathering my thoughts. "Hi Kristen," I finally managed by force of habit.

I was so thrown at having her show up, she walked right through the door while I was standing there numbly.

"Kristen, what are you doing here?" I asked.

She glanced around my townhouse. "Finn, I can't believe you found this place."

Her gaze swung back to mine. I looked at her, taking the moment to absorb her appearance. Her blonde hair was pulled back into a sleek knot, and her nails were perfectly manicured. She wore black slacks and a fitted white blouse with black flats. She was classy as ever. I could objectively see she was beautiful, quite lovely in fact. She looked as if she had lost a little bit of weight. Her cheekbones stood out more sharply than I recalled. I felt nothing in response to her. Her blue eyes were pretty, yet they didn't have the gleam Jana's almost always held. Kristen's bland, neutral presence felt monochrome in contrast to Jana's bright, bold presence.

I managed to smile politely, recalling her last comment. "Thank you. It's a nice place."

I slid my hands in my pockets and rested my shoulder against the wall by the door. I wasn't going to shove her back out, but I wasn't going to invite her to stay either.

As though she read my mind. "You're not inviting me to share tea," she said with a little giggle. "I used to love your British tea thing."

I arched a brow. "British tea thing?"

"Yes. You like tea. Men from here don't drink tea as often." She paused and looked around. I sensed if I moved even an inch away from the entryway, she'd take herself on a tour. Glancing back to me, she commented, "You haven't even decorated for Christmas."

I simply shrugged. "So I haven't. Haven't found the time. What brings you here, Kristen?" I elected to entirely ignore her attempt to cajole me into offering her some tea.

She adjusted her purse on her shoulder and clasped her hands in front of her. "I haven't seen you in a while. I thought we could get together and have dinner."

"Kristen, we broke up. You canceled the wedding. I'm all about being friendly, but I don't see any reason to get together and have dinner." I couldn't fucking believe she'd showed up and wanted to have dinner.

She sighed, cocking her head to the side. I think she thought she was being cute. I didn't really know.

"Oh come on, Finn. That's water under the bridge. Let's try to be friends," she cajoled.

I was, quite simply, irritated. Why she would think it made sense that I'd want to be friends was beyond me. I'd admit I'd become more cynical about relationships after our break up, mostly because I didn't think they were worth the bother. I supposed I could chalk that up to Kristen, but I didn't particularly want to be friends. She was a part of my life at a time in my life when my feelings were more shallow and my focus was more outward. As I stood there with Kristen, Jana sashayed into my thoughts—how alive she felt, how bursting with energy she was, the drive she carried was so powerful.

With Kristen, well, I really felt nothing right now. I could call up the old feelings I'd once had. They were warmer and softer. They definitely didn't grab me by the balls, hold my heart in a vise and make me wonder if I was losing my mind. Most definitely not.

Yet, I was a gentleman, so I managed a polite smile. "It's nice to see you, Kristen. I hope you're well, but let's allow that water to stay under the bridge."

She rested her hand on her hip. "Geez, not too friendly are you?"

"Kristen, let it go. I wish you the best. Are you seeing anyone right now?" I asked.

She rolled her eyes. "I was, but it didn't work out."

"I'm sorry to hear that."

So Eli had nailed it. She was in between relationships. I beat back the urge to state the obvious.

She was quiet, her gaze still expectant. "Do you miss playing?"

"I still play here and there. Obviously, I'm not pro, but I help coach a local team and catch games when I can." There was a local football league, excuse me soccer, here in the States, and I was fairly active with it.

Kristen nodded and reached for the door handle. Pausing, she turned back and let the truth drop. "You never told me about your trust fund," she said.

I arched a brow. "Pardon?"

"You get a trust fund when you're thirty-five, and you never told me about it," she clarified.

I gave my head a little shake, my irritation at her sudden appearance spiking again. "I didn't even know about it until after you broke things off. We were young and in university," I added as though she needed me to remind her of that detail.

It was taking most of my discipline not to swear at her and shove her out the door at this point. Why the hell was she asking about money?

"Yeah, but we were engaged, and you never even mentioned it," she explained, her brow furrowing.

Of all the things for her to be affronted about. Bloody hell.

"Kristen, we were twenty-four when you broke off our engagement. It's been years. I didn't even know what I stood to inherit until I was twenty-five. I don't really see why that matters at all now. You knew what my father did, and you knew he was well-established financially. Does this perhaps have something to do with why you're here?" I asked, my voice tight.

"I just find it odd you didn't tell me about it."

"Not bloody likely I could tell you something I didn't know about. Again, I don't see how this matters."

Two bright red spots appeared high on her cheekbones.

"I'm not sure why you're nosing around my personal finances," I added.

She huffed, actually huffed. "Whatever. I talked to your sister, and she mentioned it," she muttered.

"You talked to Sarah?"

Kristen nodded, her hand gripping the door handle tightly.

I was going to have to remind Sarah I'd rather she kept her bloody mouth shut.

"Well, now you know. I don't see what it has to do with us being friends, or anything. Please carry on with your day," I said.

I reached past her, nudging her hand off the door handle and swinging it open. I gestured for her to depart. She paused for a second, the furrow between her brows tightening as she opened her mouth. I could tell she was ready to keep arguing about whatever the fuck she wanted to argue about. I was having none of it.

"Have a good afternoon, Kristen."

I moved to close the door, and she hurried out. "God, Finn. Have some manners."

I slammed the door behind her, giving the smooth wooden surface my finger. Bloody good riddance. Why, oh why did I have to wonder again about the timing of our break up? I didn't think about it much, but after the car accident, I was a mess—physically and emotionally.

She hung around for the recovery. I didn't think she enjoyed it, but then I wouldn't have expected anybody to enjoy it. She was gone once it became clear I wouldn't be able to return to play quickly enough to be considered for the pros. Truth be told, I could've rededicated myself and maybe, just maybe, gotten back to full speed. That alone would've taken too long to be viable in the pros.

I couldn't help but wonder if Kristen had known about my trust fund back then if she'd have stayed. I was bloody relieved she hadn't known. Though she'd managed to piss me off, the feeling dissipated quickly. She was long gone, and I was damn grateful.

My phone vibrated on the kitchen counter. I strode through the living room to the island and spun it around, laughing the moment I saw the text. Jana had resumed her texting habits the last day or so. The theme seemed to be silly animal pictures. She'd just sent one of a pig wearing a tutu.

I pondered whether Jana would be the type of woman for whom money would make or break a commitment. I knew without a doubt, it wouldn't for her. It just wasn't the kind of person she was. Emotion knotted in my throat, and I quickly picked up my phone. Swiping her text to the side, I called her. She answered on the first ring.

"Hey what's up?"

"Yesterday was Thursday, and today is Friday," I said, referencing a text earlier this week. "I think we should have dinner tonight."

There was a weighted silence. I could actually feel the wheels turning in her brain through the phone.

"Okay, let's. Where do you want to meet?"

"How about I cook?"

"You cook? Thank God I'm sitting down."

I chuckled "Where are you sitting?"

"At my desk at the office."

"I think maybe I should come see you at the office. I don't know where you work though."

"Oh, you should," she said, her voice filled with glee. "I work with Zoe. I think you should come to the office right now in fact."

I needed no further instruction. "Text me the address. I'll be there as soon as I can."

Chapter Eighteen

JANA

I leapt up from my desk, galvanized at the knowledge Finn was on his way over here. I hurried over to check Zoe's office, insanely to make sure she wasn't there when I knew perfectly well she wasn't. She was gone for the rest of the day at court and then meeting Ethan to go to one of his games. I raced into the bathroom, sifting my fingers through my hair and giving myself a once over. I was looking a bit worse for the wear with my skin paler than usual and my eyes puffy from poor sleep. I'd had a long week at work, and I'd finally turned in my law school paperwork to finish next semester. As such, I'd started studying at night.

I splashed water on my face and swiped lip gloss on. My hair would have to do as it was. I had one thing on my brain —Finn. Well, make that two. Finn and sex. My attempt to keep my distance had only left me longing for him. That should've given me pause, but it didn't. I gave my head a shake and left the bathroom. Once again, I checked the door to Zoe's office, needlessly closing it. She wasn't here and wouldn't be here, but it felt funny leaving it open. I then hurried to tidy my desk. Yet another entirely needless task. I seriously doubted Finn would care about the state of my desk.

I had no idea how much time had passed since he'd called, but my body was humming in anticipation. I heard footsteps in the hallway outside of our office door. The office I shared with Zoe was in central downtown Seattle on the upper floor of an office building. We had a nice view of the harbor. In the reception area, I had a curved desk that faced the front. Behind that, I had a small office with a window that shared the pretty harbor view in the distance. I didn't actually spend much time in there, but I used it when I needed to buckle down and work on court documents. We didn't get many drop-in clients, so it wasn't necessary for me to be at the reception desk all the time.

The footsteps came to a stop outside our door, my heart rate pausing along with them. I couldn't tell whether it was Finn or not. All I could see was a blurred shape through the frosted glass blocks surrounding either side of the main door. After a moment, Finn stepped inside. One look at him and my pulse lunged and my breath caught. He was in uniform, and I could've melted on the spot. The navy looked quite good on him, almost matching his eyes now that I thought about it.

"Hi," I said, my voice coming out breathy.

His mouth hitched at one corner, a grin stretching slowly across his face. He shut the door behind him. I was standing at the corner of my desk, and I zipped across the room, locking the door behind him and leaning against it with a grin. He turned to throw a puzzled look in my direction.

"Hi," I said again, repeating my greeting and trying to will my pulse to slow down.

"Hello," he returned. "How are you?"

"Great," I managed.

He glanced around the office. Beyond the main door with frosted glass on either side lay the entry area. It was open and airy. We'd decorated it in soft grays and muted blues. My desk was a rich mahogany, curving into the wall facing the door. The bathroom was off to one side with a small waiting area to the other. There were several soft gray chairs with a low, circular table in front of them. The door to Zoe's office was beyond that.

Finn's eyes landed back on mine. "So this is just you and Zoe?" he asked.

I nodded. "It's her practice, and I'm the paralegal-slash-receptionist," I offered. "We met in law school. I'm going to finish my courses soon," I added, getting suddenly anxious about saying that out loud. I didn't know why I felt the need to explain it to him.

"Some people don't actually want to be lawyers," he commented. "I hear paralegal work can pay just as well without as much stress and less liability."

I shrugged, still leaning against the door. "True, but I was close to finishing. I only have one semester left."

"What happened?" he asked.

My heart tightened, and I swallowed. Thinking about that time was hard for me. It wasn't just everything that blew up with Rick. It was my mom dying and how the collision of events sent me into a spiral of depression. I took a deep breath, breathing through the knot in my throat.

"It's kind of complicated. I'll explain another time."

Finn stared at me, his far too perceptive gaze making me want to squirm. Restless with need coursing through my veins, I reached between us and curled my fingers into the handcuffs hanging on the edge of his belt, tugging him to me. The gravelly sound of his laugh sent a prickle down my spine and a hot shiver over the surface of my skin.

"Rain check on that topic," he said with another low chuckle.

I slid my hand up around the nape of his neck, threading my fingers into his hair and tugging him down to me. I arched up, bringing my lips up to meet his, feeling a jolt straight through to my toes at the point of contact. He took control instantly, stepping closer, crowding me against the door, his hard muscled body pressed to mine. He tangled a hand roughly in my hair, swept his tongue into my mouth and our kiss went wild.

My head thumped against the door as he angled his head to the side and devoured my mouth. I hooked a foot around his calf, arching into him and running my hands up over his shoulders, down his muscled spine and gripping his tight ass. He was hard all over, and I loved it. His knee slid between my thighs, and I rolled my hips against his thigh, chasing the sharp spikes of pleasure. He broke free from our kiss, muttering my name.

"Bloody hell, Jana. I missed you," he murmured.

His lips blazed a searing, damp trail down my neck. He yanked at my blouse, not even trying to be tidy about it. I heard a button ping against the glass beside us and then bounce off the floor. Shoving my bra out of the way, he cupped my breasts in his hands. My head bumped against the door with a low moan.

"Jana," Finn said, his voice a gruff command.

I dragged my eyes open to find his waiting, his gaze dark and hot. I swallowed. Desire was whipping through me, tightening inside my core. The anticipation, the intensity, and the longing were tangled up in the intimacy I felt when I was with him. He pinched my nipples. A sharp cry fell from my lips.

"Do that again," I demanded, craving the sharp bite of it.

With a grin, so dangerous, so sexy and doing crazy things to my insides, he obliged. He flicked his thumb on the clasp between my breasts, and they tumbled loose—hot, tight, and achy. Flutters twirled in my belly, a storm massing inside. He dipped his head, dragging his tongue in a wet path along the valley between my breasts before angling over to a nipple. He swirled his tongue around it, his teeth scoring the taut peak, as he drew it in his mouth. The wet suction alone sent flares of pleasure shooting through me. I rolled my hips against his knee, restless and impatient, the sensation driving me so intense I needed to find relief.

All he did was drive me wilder. His tongue made its way over to my other nipple, the sharp bite of his teeth barely easing the need lashing at me as he bit down. I yanked at the buttons of the shirt, sighing when I could feel the hard planes of his chest, his skin hot against me. When I dipped my head and dragged my tongue along his skin, he muttered something and then lifted me roughly against him. He spun around and took several quick strides, sliding my hips onto my desk. My skirt conveniently rode up my thighs. He stepped back, dragging my hips close to the edge.

His eyes flicked to mine. I tried to tug him to me, but he shook his head. He knelt between my knees, dragging a single finger over the wet silk there. When he pushed my thighs apart, the cool air hitting the wet heat there sent a shiver through me. Another tease of his fingers over the silk and then he brought his mouth to me, right through the silk, drawing his tongue over it and sucking my clit. I cried out, the pleasure sharp and deep, echoing through my body.

"Finn, don't make me wait..."

My words trailed out with a gasp.

He drew back, his eyes flicking to mine. "Oh, you'll wait. You made me wait for days," he muttered with a rough chuckle, teasing me through the now soaking wet silk.

After a moment, he reached up and yanked my panties down. I lifted my hips to help, kicking them free. He spread my folds apart. My sex clenched and throbbed as he teased me, dragging his fingers back and forth through the slick wetness, grazing over my clit. Just when I thought I might die, he sank a finger inside.

I scrambled, gripping my hands on the edge of the desk behind me as I leaned back. I was wanton and wild, my skirt hiked up around my hips, my blouse falling open, and desperate for him to be inside of me. He said he would make me wait, yet he neglected to mention he would drive me to the edge of sanity while he was at it. Another finger joined the first, and he set to stroking in and out of me. Just when I thought I couldn't take it anymore, he brought his mouth to me again, sucking my clit in and sending me hurtling over the edge with such force, my elbows gave out and I fell against the desk.

He drew away slowly. I heard him unbuttoning his slacks, and I rose up.

"I need you. Now," I demanded.

"Right here," he replied, his voice tight.

Gripping his cock, hard and thick, in his fist, he slid the head of it through my folds, slippery wet now. I curled my legs around his hips and arched into him. In one swift surge, he sank inside, seating himself deeply in my core. The sensation of him filling me was so good, so right, I cried out. He held still for beat.

"Jana," he said, my name another gruff command.

I rose up on my elbows again, locking my eyes to his. It felt overwhelming, but I couldn't look away. He drew back slowly, looking down between us. My gaze followed his to see his cock, glistening wet, as he drew back and then sank inside of me again and again. We watched together, the sight so arousing, I nearly came again. But then he spoke my name and laced a hand in my hair, leaning forward as he sank deeply to the hilt. With one hand curling around my hip and holding me close, he brought his lips to mine and caught my cries in our kiss. My orgasm started at my toes and rolled through me, so deep and intense, it rang every chord of every fiber in my being. I felt his release as he went taut, the heat of it filling me.

We pulsed together, and then he slowly drew back. We stared at each other, our breath heaving. After a moment, he sifted his fingers through my hair, tracing his thumb along my jaw and then around my lips. I caught it in my teeth, releasing it gently. I wanted to cry, but it wasn't the bad kind of tears.

The emotion welling up was so intense, I didn't know what to do with it, so I pushed against it and forced myself to be light.

"So dinner you said?"

He held my gaze, his eyes searching, and then he nodded. "So I did. Dinner then."

He slowly drew out of me, and I missed the connection instantly. Ever the gentleman, he helped me put my clothes back in place. As we walked out of the office, hand in hand, I wondered if I'd lost my mind. Or better yet, my heart.

FINN

I woke to the feel of a furry face rubbing against mine and the sound of purring. For a moment, I was confused and then I recalled where I was—in Jana's bed. Smokey had taken this opportunity to greet me. I reached up and stroked him for a moment before he leapt off the bed, and I heard him scurrying out of the bedroom. Jana was warm against my side, her breathing steady and even. Her head was tucked against my shoulder, and one of her legs was thrown across mine. Her curves were soft against me, her skin like silk. I glanced to her, the streetlights through the window limning her features. Her hair was a tangle around her face.

My mind spun back to last night. After our interlude in her office, we'd stopped by my place so I could change out of my uniform and then went to the grocery store to gather ingredients for dinner. Upon her request, we made a stir fry. I loved to cook. I always had. Perhaps it was because the kitchen was where I spent the most time with my mother growing up. She'd lug me into the kitchen with her, along with my younger sister, who'd rebelled and declared she hated cooking. As a bachelor, it was a bonus to be able to cook halfway decent meals for myself.

After dinner, we'd lounged on Jana's sofa. When she'd fallen asleep, I'd carried her into the bedroom. She'd come awake long enough to strip herself bare and collapse against me, warm and naked. My mind ran in circles in my brain, wondering just what I was getting myself into with Jana. I liked her. I liked her so much, I was dancing along the edges of thinking there was more to it. Yet, I wasn't quite sure what to think. I hadn't intended for this to be anything more than yet another casual fling, though I can't say I thought much about it. My draw to Jana had been too powerful to ignore, and yet trying to consider more wasn't simple. Trust didn't come easily to me.

I wanted to relax, but I didn't know if I could. Yet, right now, Jana was warm beside me, and I didn't want to think about anything else. She shifted in her sleep, and I slid my palm down her back, savoring the warmth of her skin and letting my hand come to rest on the lush curve of her bottom. On the heels of another deep breath, I fell back to sleep.

I woke the following morning, instantly sensing Jana wasn't in bed with me. I rolled to the side to see steam billowing out of the bathroom door. I sat up swiftly and strode into the shower. The moment I stepped in and saw her there, bare naked with soap bubbles rolling over her skin, my cock hardened. There was no such thing as being partially aroused around Jana. I was rock hard and ready. I stepped behind her, sliding my hands down her sides, savoring the soft curves of her breasts, the dip at her waist and the flare of her hips.

She gasped, a little squeak coming out. I didn't even bother to hide my arousal, stepping against her and savoring the feel of her luscious bottom against my cock. She giggled and lifted her face to rinse it before spinning in my arms.

Her eyes were bright with her dark hair slicked away from her face and her damp lashes.

"Good morning," she said with a sly grin, reaching between us and curling her palm around my cock.

"Morning," I murmured in return, dipping my head and meaning to kiss her.

But she shimmied down, glancing up to me and dragging her tongue along my cock, swirling it around the head. My cock throbbed, so hard for her it ached. I watched as her mouth closed around the head of my cock and she drew me inside, her eyes on me the whole time. She slid back, the suction sending a jolt of need through me.

Fisting my cock in her wet grip, she drew me in again and again. She released me only to cup my balls as she took me in deeply, the head of my cock bumping against the back of her throat. Bloody hell. Jana sucking me off was about the best way to wake up I could even imagine. A few more deep strokes as she teased me, and I couldn't take it anymore. I needed to be inside of her.

I murmured her name roughly as I reached for her, dragging her up, and spinning her around. Her palms slapped against the tile wall. As if she could read my mind, she knew what I wanted. She spread her thighs apart and arched her back. I slid my palm down the sweet dip of her spine and over the luscious curve of her bottom. I gripped her hip in one hand, my cock in the other, dragging it through the wet folds. She was slick and ready. I sank into her, seating myself deeply in her creamy clench. She cried out, arching back into me.

I took her roughly, pounding into her. I gripped both of her hips as I held her in place, drumming into her, her pussy clenching around me and milking my cock. I reached around, stroking over her swollen nub, gritting my teeth and hanging onto my restraint until I felt her moan and let go around me. Her sex clamped down, and I finally let go.

My release thundered through me, whipping through me

so hard my palm slapped against the tile beside her to keep from collapsing. We held still together with me curled over her, our breath heaving as hot water poured down over us. As the pounding slowly eased inside, I uncurled and drew back slowly, spinning her in my arms and finally kissing her.

When I pulled away with my hand tangled in her wet hair and cupping her bottom to hold her close, my heart tightened as I stared into the deep blue of her eyes. I forced myself to step back and lighten the moment. I reached for the soap and handed it to her with a grin. I felt emotionally rattled and sensed the same from her.

"Morning luv," I managed, striving for a light, teasing tone.

She returned my grin and threw the bar of soap at me. After we showered and were getting dressed, I felt somewhat more grounded.

"That was a sufficiently nice way to wake up," she said with a laugh.

"Sufficiently nice?" I countered, narrowing my eyes.

She flashed a grin. "Okay. It was amazing."

She pulled a shirt over her head, her voice muffled. "Are you working today?"

When her face reappeared, I shook my head as I buttoned my jeans. "Nope. You?" I asked.

"I don't usually work Saturdays. Here and there, I might do some extra paperwork or court filings, but I'm all caught up. Should we do something today?"

I held her gaze, contemplating her question. It had been years since I'd done much more than dinner and sex with a woman. So I shrugged. "I don't know. Is there something you'd like to do?" I asked.

I might not know what to do, but I knew I didn't want to leave her side. Not just yet.

"Let's go to the beach."

Chapter Twenty

JANA

We stood on the beach, staring out over the water. The day had started sunny, but it was slightly overcast now. The ocean was calm today, stretching into the distance—a sea, not a metaphorical one, but an actual one, of slate gray water ruffled softly by the wind. Rocks rose up through the mist over to one side. Seagulls called and swooped through the air. We were standing on a beach just beyond an old favorite place of mine. I took a deep breath, savoring the salty scent. Simply being by the ocean itself felt freeing as the wind washed away my worries.

Finn had gamely come along with me, declaring in his proper British accent that he hadn't been out here before. He'd only visited the ocean along the harbor in Seattle. We were just north of Saltwater State Park at a local beach. I used to come here often with my mother when I was little. I was taking Finn to brunch at one of my favorite places. I spun away from the view and grabbed his hand.

"Come on. I'm starving."

Within minutes, he followed my directions and rolled to a stop in front of Sal's Diner. It was an old diner in a weathered square building with faded silver flashing on the roof. I loved this place, and they had the best biscuits and gravy ever.

"Best biscuits and gravy," I announced as I perused the menu once we were sated.

"Biscuits and gravy?" he repeated, arching a brow. "That's an American thing, isn't it?"

"Yes, and it's the best. If you haven't had it, you have to get it."

His mouth curled at the corner, that sexy grin of his sending my belly into a tailspin of flutters.

"I have to?"

"Yes," I declared, nudging his wrist with the corner of my menu.

Finn chuckled, his low laugh sending a shiver through me, and shrugged. "Very well then. I shall."

"Good." I leaned back in my seat, sliding my hand along the red vinyl of the booth seat.

I watched as he looked around the restaurant. It was a classic, basic diner with booths lining the walls of the small space. A counter ran the length of the back wall with stools. The kitchen was immediately behind the counter with the grill in full view. Sal and June Torro owned this place. They were old friends of my mother's. I'd never brought any man here, and I didn't know quite what I was thinking, but it was the only place I'd wanted to go today.

A Christmas tree was tucked into a corner at the end of the counter with a hodgepodge of decorations. Sal and June let the local elementary school decorate the tree every year, which meant hordes of small children bouncing around the tree and a wide variation in how it looked from year to year. One side of this year's tree was heavily weighted with decorations, but the glitter and bows on the other side balanced it out.

Sal hadn't been behind the counter when we arrived. Our waitress came by to fill our coffees, and Finn politely ordered the biscuits and gravy with a side of hash after I did. Our waitress, Mabel, looked to me with a warm smile as she collected our menus.

"Sal's in the back. I'll tell him you're here," she offered as she walked away.

Finn arched a brow in question. I was coming to love how he stayed engaged in conversation without ever being pushy. I couldn't say the same about myself.

"Sal's an old family friend," I explained.

He simply nodded and then asked the obvious next question. "Where is your family anyway? Do they live around here then?"

I swallowed against the emotion that suddenly clogged my throat. I was an only child, raised by my mother. My dad had been, well he just hadn't been around. I knew who he was, and he was still alive. He'd never paid a dime in child support, and we didn't have much of a relationship. I gave Finn the answer that I'd trained myself to say ever since my mother had died. "It was just me and my mom. She passed away a few years ago."

I still hated that answer. Because we'd been close, and I missed her so damn much.

"I'm sorry," he said simply, his eyes warm, searching my face. I sensed he was trying to assess how upset I might be.

"Thank you. It's okay. It sucks, but you do get used to it." I gave myself a shake. "Anyway, Sal and his wife were good friends of hers, so I still come here," I offered, suddenly realizing that this place might seem to have more meaning than I wanted him to consider.

Sal conveniently saved me, coming out through the swinging doors beside the kitchen and calling my name as he walked across the room. "Jana girl," he said in his gruff voice.

My heart softened the moment I saw him. I adored Sal. He was round and portly with gray hair. His twinkling brown eyes crinkled at the corners with his smile when he reached us. I stood to give him a quick hug. He squeezed me tight and then set me back, sliding his hands down over my shoulders and squeezing my hands as I slipped into the booth.

"Hey Sal," I said.

"It's been too long. I was just saying to June the other night that I wondered how you were doing," he replied.

"Well, here I am. Is June around this morning?"

Sal shook his head. "No, she took Dots to the vet," he replied, referring to their dog.

"Oh, is Dots okay?"

"She's just getting her shots. Nothing to worry about. June will be here in a little bit. How long will you be here?"

"Long enough to finish breakfast," I offered.

I felt his curious gaze flick from me to Finn.

I glanced from Finn to Sal. "Sal, this is Finn, and Finn, this is Sal," I offered, gesturing between them.

Finn stood and reached to shake Sal's hand. Sal sized him up, his gaze skeptical. I supposed it was an event for me to bring a man here. In many ways, Sal was the closest thing I had to a father.

"Nice to meet you, sir," Finn said.

"You as well," Sal returned before glancing to me as he released Finn's hand. "What's a British lad doing here?" he asked.

Finn's answer came smoothly. "I attended university here and stayed," he offered simply. His explanation barely scratched the surface of the story, but it was the truth.

Sal nodded and then embarrassed the hell out of me. "Are you her boyfriend?" he asked sharply.

Finn had just returned to his seat and taken a sip of his coffee. He almost choked on it. He gaze bounced to me as he reached for a napkin.

I caught Sal's eyes. "We had dinner last night, and we're here for breakfast. Get over it. I'm an adult and have been for years."

Sal narrowed his eyes at me. "I know you're an adult, but you don't have anybody to look out after you, so I figure I better," he declared without the slightest bit of shame about being nosy.

Finn chuckled politely, looking from me to Sal. "I would expect someone to do that, although I daresay Jana can take rather good care of herself," he said politely.

Sal grinned. "I like you lad. She can take rather good care of herself. If anything, she's a bit prickly."

There was a softness behind Sal's sarcasm. Finn chuckled, his eyes bouncing to mine. I saw the understanding flickering in the depths of his eyes, and it made me feel funny. My heart gave a little skip. Emotion welled in my chest. I felt ways I'd never expected to feel. Trust didn't come easily for me after everything blew up with Rick. Trying to date was annoying enough. It was difficult to trust anyone, and yet somehow I trusted Finn.

"So what did you order for breakfast?" Sal asked, conveniently nudging the conversation along.

"Biscuits and gravy," Finn said with a grin.

"Ah, Jana's favorite. Have you had it before?" Sal asked.

"Can't say I have. It's not that I haven't been to diners here in the States. I just haven't gotten around to trying it."

Sal winked. "You'll like it."

Someone called Sal's name from the kitchen. He gave my shoulder a squeeze and leaned over to drop a kiss on my cheek. "Try to come back soon and let us know you're coming, so June can see you." He threw a glance to Finn. "Nice meeting you. Take good care of her."

At that, he hurried away, pushing through the swinging doors. The sounds from the kitchen behind the grill filtered out into the diner. I took a fortifying sip of my coffee and caught Finn's eyes. "Sorry he put you on the spot. Sal's kind of like... Well, I don't know, I guess he's kind of the closest thing I ever had to a father."

My words slipped out and then my cheeks heated. My added explanation stumbled out on its own. "It was just me and my mom. My dad was never really around. June was one of her good friends from growing up, so she and Sal babysat for me a lot. We did holidays with them."

Finn's gaze was steady. He was gracious enough to accept that explanation and not ask for more. He took a measured swallow of his coffee before setting it down and adding a dash of cream. "It's nice to have people like that. Family isn't always simple."

"No. I don't suppose it ever is. Where's your family?" I asked, shifting the topic away from myself.

"London," he offered.

I knew a bit from Ethan, but I wanted to hear it from Finn.

"Both of my parents are still alive. My father runs an investment company, and my mother was a teacher, although she's retired now."

"Any brothers or sisters?"

"I have one younger sister. Sarah."

"Is she in London as well?"

He shook his head. "Oh no. Sarah never stays in one place for long. At the moment, she's in Washington, DC. You might meet her because she texted me to say she might be out for a visit in the next few weeks for the holidays."

I nodded along politely, curious to know what Finn's sister would be like. As I contemplated this, I realized we were doing what people did when they were something more than casual. I shoved those thoughts away quickly.

In short order, we had our biscuits and gravy. I took a bite, moaning at the delicious flavor. It was homey and comforting and perfect. I glanced across the table to Finn to find his eyes on me, darkening.

He tapped his finger at the corner of his mouth. "You missed some gravy."

I slipped my tongue out, curling it to capture the lost drop of gravy. His eyes darkened further, and my pulse responded in kind, heat flashing through me. Sweet hell. All he had to do was look at me, and I got hot and bothered. It didn't seem to matter I should be sated after our interlude this morning.

"What do you think?" I asked.

I forced myself to pause eating. After taking a bite, he held my gaze and then nodded firmly. "Delicious. It appears I've missed out not trying this sooner. I admit I was confused when I first heard the name of the dish."

"What do you mean?"

"Biscuits are cookies in Britain," he explained.

"Oh, like the sweet kind?"

At his nod, I burst out laughing. "Oh my god! No wonder you were confused."

He grinned as he took another bite, tucking in to eat. Sal came over to check on us as we were leaving. Finn insisted on paying and wouldn't let me argue the point. Sal didn't help.

"Oh hush. He gets to pay." Sal enveloped me in a big hug on our way out, and clapped Finn on the shoulder, which was high praise from Sal. He could be a standoffish sort of man.

As we walked outside, I meant to tell Finn we should drive back to Seattle. I didn't.

"We should go back to the beach for a walk."

Chapter Twenty-One

FINN

A few days later, I walked down the hallway at the court-house, pausing at the door that led to the attorneys' offices. When I flashed my badge, the security guard nodded from the window behind and let me through.

"Here to see Becca?" he called out as I passed by his open doorway.

"That I am. Is she in her office?" I asked in return. At his nod, I kept moving, making my way to Becca's office.

I rapped my knuckles on Becca's door. When she called out for me to come in, I stepped inside, closing the door behind me and muting the cacophony from the hallway. The District Attorney's office in Seattle was always bustling and today was no exception.

Becca looked up from her desk. She was rarely frazzled, although today she looked on the verge of it. Her dark hair was pulled back in a knot and her blue eyes were snapping. She finished a phone call, setting the phone down and throwing a glare at it.

"Good morning, Finn," she said in a syrupy sweet voice

as if in attempt to counteract her annoyance at whoever had been on the phone.

"Morning Becca. I saw the news crew outside. I would suppose they're here for Ray's hearing."

She rolled her eyes. "I would suppose. I spoke to Lynne Sutton this morning. She's holding up okay. Stressed, but okay. Have you had a chance to talk to her?"

"I called over this morning as well. She'll be here. Her family's hired an attorney to help support her."

"We have a solid case," Becca said firmly.

"That we do. It shall be fine once we get through with court."

Becca's cell phone rang. Glancing down at her phone screen, her gaze softened. "Hang on. Let me take this." She spun away. Her conversation was brief. I heard the end as she turned back. "Love you, I'll be home by seven."

I surmised that was her husband. Only seconds on the phone with him, and she looked more relaxed. "How is Aidan?" I asked.

Becca flashed a smile. "He's fine. He's worried I'm working too much."

"Aren't you?" I countered.

She rolled her eyes. "Maybe. He works hard too though."

"No doubt. Once you have your baby, perhaps you'll slow down."

Becca cocked her head to the side. "I know. We'll see how that goes. I can't decide."

"Decide about what?"

"Whether or not to cut my hours back once we have the baby. What do you think?"

Startled at her question, I was flummoxed for a beat before I replied. "I think that's between you and Aidan, don't you?"

Becca chuckled. "I suppose. Aidan volunteered to cut his hours back, but I think I'd feel guilty."

I nodded if only because I had no idea what else to say. I knew Becca well enough, yet not well enough to offer an opinion on how to handle work and babies.

"Speaking of settling down, what about you?" she asked.

"What about me?"

"You're handsome, you've got that hot British accent, you have a steady job and you're actually nice. You are, as they say, a catch," she said with a slight grin. "Should I set you up with one of my friends?"

The horror must've shown on my face because she threw her head back with a laugh. Her gaze sobered as her laugh petered out. "No seriously, you're a nice guy. You'd make a great husband."

Unprepared for this turn in our conversation, I simply nodded again and shifted in my seat.

"Are you seeing anyone?" Becca asked, nudging me a little more on the topic than I wanted to be nudged.

"What's with you this morning? Getting rather personal, aren't we?"

"Oh, cut it out. I know you well enough to ask. I don't mean to imply you *should* settle down, but I can't imagine you being alone for the rest of your life. You're not really bachelor material."

I must've looked confused because she continued. "You're nice, you're stable, and as far as I know, you don't have a bad reputation as a jerk or a heartbreaker. You're discreet..."

I cut in. "What does being discreet have to do with it?"

"Oh, I don't know. It just means you're not openly an asshole, or arrogant and flaunting gorgeous women all the time," she clarified.

I chuckled. "Fair enough. I suppose I should say thanks."

Becca grinned. "Anyway, are you seeing anyone?"

Jana sashayed into my thoughts. I supposed I was seeing her, in a way I hadn't *seen* anyone in years. I didn't know what to call what we were to each other. It was as if a ball had started rolling, and we couldn't stop it. After we had brunch at Sal's Diner over the weekend, she took me to what she declared was her favorite beach for a walk. We spent a few hours there, and on the way back to Seattle, we stopped and had an early dinner. It was the second weekend in a row where I'd spent both nights with her.

Considering that now, I tried to remember the last time I'd spent two weekends in a row with any woman. It hadn't been since Kristen and I had been together. I started to panic slightly every time I thought about it. Take now for example, I pushed the thoughts away because the one thing I didn't want to do was stop seeing Jana.

Rather than answering Becca's question if I was seeing anyone, I asked, "How long have you and Aidan been married?"

Becca drummed her fingertips on the table, a smile unfurling. "Four years."

"Does it get old?" I asked in return.

She laughed softly. "I'm not sure what you mean by that. You get comfortable—both good and bad comfortable—in the sense that I know all of his annoying habits and he knows mine. There are things I can count on every day, and I don't mean the big stuff. I mean the small stuff, like if I wake up with a headache, he gets me ibuprofen and tea before I even think to ask. He nags me about working too much, and I do the same to him. It's only been four years, but I've already figured out we have to work on it. Not in the sense of loving him, but remembering that you can't be with somebody day in and day out and not try. Why do you ask?"

I held her gaze for a few beats. "I suppose I'm seeing someone," I finally explained.

She smiled softly. "I want to tease you, but I'm guessing you wouldn't be saying anything if this someone didn't matter."

I shrugged. The moment Becca shared her observation, I

knew it to be dead on. Jana mattered. *A lot*. Yet, I wasn't certain I was prepared to face what that meant.

"Dunno. It's not something I've considered for a long time."

Becca nodded slowly, keeping her gaze trained on me. "Rumor has it you've been a dedicated bachelor ever since your engagement broke up. Tell me about her. Who is she?"

I looked over at Becca, Jana waltzing through my thoughts—with her rich brown hair and streaks of bright color, her gorgeous blue eyes, usually with a glimpse of mirth in them, her lopsided smile and the bold, funny way she raced at life, I was finding it near impossible not to think about her. I pondered those few times when I saw vulnerability flickering in the depths of her gaze. Simply thinking about it tightened my heart. I cleared my throat and caught Becca's eyes, schooling my expression to calm.

"Jana, Jana Sparks," I said.

Becca cocked her head to the side. "Oh, isn't she the paralegal for Zoe Walsh?"

I should've guessed Becca would know who Jana was. Becca had likely crossed paths with Zoe in court. "Yes, she is. She's finishing up her law courses next semester."

Becca was quiet, her gaze reflective.

"What's that look for?" I asked.

She shrugged. "Oh, I don't know Jana well, but there were some nasty rumors about her a few years ago. None of it her fault. I just felt bad for her at the time."

She must've been referring to Jana's comment about what happened after her relationship with Rick, or rather the bloody arse as I thought of him.

"What rumors?" I asked, curious to hear about it from someone other than Jana.

Becca shrugged softly and sighed. "She got involved with her old boss. It was a big to-do because he was married. She lost her job and lost a bunch of job opportunities because of it. I knew Rick was a fucking asshole. He had tons of affairs.

He also had a nasty habit of having affairs with women who didn't know he was married. Thank God his wife finally divorced him. Anyway, I just felt bad for Jana about the whole thing. I'm not saying it was smart to hook up with her boss, but the rest of it she didn't know. One thing I hate about our world is how men get away with being the assholes, and women get blasted. Even if the situation had been reversed, Jana's was the one whose reputation would've taken a hit. Aside from his wife finally telling him to fuck off, Rick came through unscathed. I was glad Jana landed on her feet working for Zoe. I think they're good friends."

I nodded. "They are. Jana mentioned that mess. It's bullshit."

"It sure is," Becca replied, her tone resigned.

A fierce sense of protectiveness rolled through me. I didn't like hearing Jana had been the subject of nasty gossip. She hadn't shied away from being honest about what happened. I wasn't sure I could say much else about it, other than to swear Rick to hell.

"Well, she seems to be in a good place now with Zoe, and she's finishing up her own law degree."

"You know what she plans to do when she's done?" Becca asked.

"I think she plans to work with Zoe."

Becca sagged into her chair. "Of course. Now, I'll have another kick ass criminal defense attorney to deal with."

I chuckled. "Not so sure she'll handle your kind of cases."

Becca flashed a grin. "Nah. Probably not. Zoe usually steers clear of DV stuff. She's a bad ass though, and I'm sure Jana will be one too."

I chuckled. Jana was already a bad ass. Her bold, charge at life attitude was part of what drew me to her so powerfully. I could only imagine she'd be a headache for prosecutors. She was sharp, witty and likely wouldn't back down from a court battle.

Becca's phone rang just as there was a knock at her door.

She looked to me, nodding towards the door as she answered the phone. "Mind getting that?" she asked before greeting her caller.

I stood to open the door to find Aidan there with two coffees in hand.

"Hello," I said, gesturing him inside the office. "I'm guessing Becca's expecting you."

Based on the look on her face, I took that as a no. Aidan chuckled as he glanced from me to her. Her eyes narrowed as she spoke to whoever was on the phone. She ended the call quickly and looked over at him. Aidan had stepped inside her office and was leaning just beside the door.

He flashed a grin. "You sounded tired, so I brought coffee."

"I see that. I'm not supposed to have much," Becca said with a grin.

"It's the smallest size they had," he countered.

I slid my hands in my pockets and nodded to Aidan. "I was just about to head out. Good to see you."

Aidan nodded quickly. "You too. I'm guessing you're here for the Sutton hearing."

Becca glared at him. "How do you...?"

Aidan rolled his eyes. "Hon, Ray Sutton is running for mayor. It's been all over the news this morning."

He stepped away from the wall and rounded her desk, setting her coffee down and leaning over to drop a lingering kiss on her cheek. Aidan McNamara ran one of the premier security companies in Seattle. He was a former Navy SEAL and looked the part. He tended to look rather foreboding, but he had a soft spot, namely Becca.

I took a moment to say my goodbyes. As I was closing the door behind me, I caught sight of Becca standing and threading her hand into Aidan's hair. I wondered what it be would be like to have Jana look at me the way Becca looked at Aidan. She so clearly adored him. Like Jana, Becca was a bold, confident woman. Yet, she softened around Aidan, as he did around her.

I gave my head a shake, forcing my attention to the moment. I didn't need to be obsessing about Jana. Yet, unless something else held my attention, Jana was waiting in the wings.

Chapter Twenty-Two

JANA

I sat on my desk, swinging my legs and laughing with Daisy Wells. Zoe and I had gotten to know her through her connection to Ethan. I'd actually been friends with her before she'd fallen head over heels in love with Tristan, an old friend of Ethan's. Daisy was a medical researcher—brilliant, beautiful, and funny as hell. I shook my head at her.

"I cannot believe you did that."

"Why? I swear Jeff Miller drives me nuts. He asked me out once before Tristan and I got together. He's so fucking annoying. He's the classic arrogant doctor. He thinks any hot woman will want him," Daisy declared with a roll of her eyes.

"What did you do?" Zoe asked, walking out of her office. Our office was closing up, and Daisy had swung by to round us up for drinks with friends.

"Oh, after my friend at work turned him down—again— I offered to set him up with someone."

"Oh God, who did you set him up with?" Zoe asked.

Daisy grinned. "Helena Stepanov."

Zoe's eyes widened. "I can't believe you did that."

Helena Stepanov was a medical researcher we knew in

passing through Daisy's position. She was model gorgeous and slightly terrifying.

"She scares the hell out of me, and that's not easy," I said.

Daisy winked. "I know, right? She kind of intimidates me too. I knew he would go for it because she's hot. I doubt he's prepared for what she's really like. Last guy she went out with, she screamed at him right in the restaurant. Her temper is legendary."

Zoe shook her head with a laugh and snagged her jacket off the coat rack by the door. I slipped my hips off the desk, the motion reminding me of the last time I sat on this desk. Finn had been buried deep inside of me on that very desk. I flushed and turned away, grabbing my jacket off of my chair. Zoe probably wouldn't appreciate the fact I'd let Finn fuck me senseless here. Well, maybe she wouldn't care. She was no prude. I also knew for a fact she had gotten wild with Ethan in her own office.

It was odd for me not to be sharing with her much about what was happening with Finn. I normally had no trouble being quite open about my dating life. Yet, I didn't want to talk about Finn. Rather, it was more that talking about Finn led to thinking about how he me feel and *that* was making me feel a little crazy. Instead, I was telling myself to relax and have fun. That had been Zoe's advice after all.

We walked out with Daisy. We were meeting two more friends, Olivia and Harper, at a nearby restaurant, 13 Coins. 13 Coins was a Seattle favorite. It had everything from classic diner food to high-end entrées. It was perfect for a night out with friends.

A short walk later, we were ensconced in a tall, leather backed booth in the restaurant. I was enjoying a pomegranate martini while we caught up with each other. Olivia, Daisy and Harper had grown up together in a town outside of Seattle. Olivia was a well-known orthopedic surgeon and had been the initial connection to the Seattle Stars when her husband, Liam Reed, ended up under her knife for knee surgery. His public declaration of love during an interview had been all over the news. Once I got to know her, I found her to be brilliant and kind. She could be on the uptight side, but she was a good counterpoint to Liam who was a tease. With her dark curls and bright green eyes, she was lovely and a contrast to Daisy's blonde hair and wide brown eyes.

Harper, with her glossy brown hair and bright blue eyes, was measured and thoughtful and had a sly sense of humor. She was married to Alex Gordon, the legendary goalkeeper for the Seattle Stars. I felt lucky to have smart, funny and amazing friends like them, yet I occasionally felt slightly *less than* when I was around them. If only, because I had never finished my law degree and they were all so respectively accomplished.

Harper was a physical therapist and had once commiserated with me about understanding what it was like to have academics go sideways. She had been raped in college by a fellow athlete, and the experience delayed her graduation. I didn't quite think my mother's death and being made a public fool by a man was quite the same as what she experienced. When I had said as much to Harper, she had merely smiled softly and commented that everyone had their own challenges, and you never knew what people were facing. I continued to be amazed at how strong she was. Considering Harper's life now, it was hard to imagine what she'd once been through.

Daisy was regaling us with the latest about her daughter Lily. "The other day, I turn around to find her drawing on the wall with crayons. She took it very specifically when I said she couldn't paint on the wall. When I told her to stop and took the crayons from her, she pointed out that crayons weren't paint. God help me," Daisy said with a laugh.

Olivia leaned back, rubbing her round belly. She was pregnant, quite pregnant actually. "That's what I'm afraid of if we have a son who's anything like Liam. According to his mother, he was a wild child."

I grinned. "You married him, he couldn't have been that bad."

Olivia shook her head. "His mother said he was a nightmare."

Daisy laughed. "Well, at least he'll have spirit, right?"

Olivia rolled her eyes. "Sure."

I looked over to Harper and Zoe. "What's the plan for you two?"

Zoe sighed, nudging me with her elbow. "Don't even ask. Just because I turned thirty, all of a sudden, it's like everybody has a license to ask when I'm having a baby."

Harper nodded vigorously. "Exactly. What if I don't want to have a baby? What if I don't know? It's like we're supposed to know way in advance."

"Don't you want a baby?" Daisy asked immediately.

I bit back a laugh at her obvious attempt to get under Harper's skin.

Harper glared at her. "I don't know. I think I do. I'm just not ready yet."

Zoe chimed in. "Stupid biological clock. Ethan's getting impatient, and I told him he needs to relax. I'm the one who actually has to have the baby," she said with a roll of her eyes.

"Hell yes," Olivia nodded firmly. "It's your decision. I mean, I'm not saying you shouldn't have a conversation about it, but let me tell you, it's no picnic. I'm eight months pregnant and some days I just want to sleep all day. I feel like a beached whale when I lay down."

Daisy almost spewed her drink all over the table.

Olivia sipped her water. "I can't wait to have an alcoholic beverage again. I told Liam that he'd better bring me a drink as soon as I give birth."

Daisy laughed. "Sorry hon. After that, you'll be nursing."

Olivia sighed. "I know. Obviously, I was kidding."

"Oh, it's not totally out of the question. You can drink and express the milk before you nurse again," Daisy added.

"Are you serious?" Zoe asked.

Daisy nodded as she took a sip of her martini. "Yep. There's even a calculation on how much to expel before it's safe to say you're nursing them with nonalcoholic breast milk. You just wait until you have a baby. You'll be talking about your body all the time."

Our waiter arrived at the part where Daisy said *nonalcoholic breast milk*. She greeted him with a wide smile after she finished speaking. His lips twitched as he paused beside our booth, glancing around the table.

"Okay ladies, have you decided on your orders?"

After he took our orders and turned to the next table, I leaned back into my seat. Zoe glanced my way, a wry grin curling the corners of her mouth. "So we're all up-to-date on the baby status. What's your status?"

"Well, I'm definitely not planning to have a baby anytime soon," I said with a little laugh. I felt my cheeks heat because I knew where she was going with her question, but I preferred to play dumb.

Unfortunately, Zoe wasn't letting me off the hook. "That's not what I meant. Do you plan to be single forever?"

Annoyed, I got snippy. "Who cares if I do? Just like people shouldn't constantly ask about babies, they shouldn't constantly look at a woman near thirty and assume she's dying to settle down."

Zoe wrinkled her nose. "Oh my God. You know that's not what I think."

Daisy immediately jumped in. "Wow, sounds like someone's a little touchy."

I rolled my eyes, crossing my legs and trying to ignore the subtle unease rising inside. "Just like babies, I get to decide whether I want to settle down or not," I said firmly.

Daisy angled her head to the side. "What's up? I was kinda joking, but you *are* a bit touchy."

"Just that," I said, wishing Daisy wasn't so persistent.

Zoe cleared her throat, way too obviously.

Olivia narrowed her eyes. "Something's up. You might as well say what."

"Fine. I might've gone on a few dates with someone."

I didn't know if what I'd done with Finn every night I spent with him was a *date*. It seemed a rather insufficient word to describe the most intimate nights I'd ever spent with anyone, each one topping the last. I shifted uncomfortably in my seat.

"With who?" Olivia asked, arching a brow.

"Finn Connors," Zoe said.

Olivia looked puzzled, but Zoe jumped in to fill in the blanks. "Ethan knows Finn. He used to play football at university, but he was injured in a car accident and never went back to it. He's a cop now, and his family has gobs of money. He *really* likes Jana."

My cheeks had to be neon red at this point. I took a deep breath and let it out slowly, glaring at Zoe before I took a big gulp of my martini. "That's what Zoe thinks," I said.

"Well, how serious is it?" Daisy asked.

Daisy was a loyal, funny friend, and I adored her. She was also persistent as hell. Sadly, if I was being honest with myself, she reminded me of myself. At this particular moment, that wasn't so great.

"I don't know if it's serious," I finally muttered, masking my annoyance with myself with a sip of my drink.

"How do you feel?" Daisy asked, ever persistent.

I shifted in my seat again and ignored the anxiety blooming in my chest. "I like him," I finally said before taking another sip of my drink. "I'm not so sure that's a good thing."

Harper caught my eyes, her gaze warm as if she sensed my discomfort. "Maybe you need a little more time to figure it out," she said.

Daisy started to open her mouth again, and Harper gave

her a look. Harper was the only one of us who could shut Daisy up.

Daisy rolled her eyes and stuck her tongue out at Harper. "Fine. I guess you want me to back off."

Harper's shoulders shook with her laughter. "Yes, give her a little space. If she wants to take things further with Finn, she will when she's ready," Harper said.

All of the feelings I'd been trying to ignore were rushing to the fore right now, fists banging on the doors of my heart.

"Or maybe she wants some advice," Olivia added.

Olivia fell somewhere in the middle between Harper and Daisy, not quite as reserved as Harper, but not quite as bold and pushy as Daisy.

"I'm not sure I need advice. I need to figure out what I want," I said bluntly.

"What do you want then?" Daisy asked, taking that as another opening.

"She just said she needed to figure that out," Harper interjected.

I bit my lip to keep from laughing at Daisy. "She's right," I offered. "I don't know."

"Well, you better figure it out. Is he a good guy?" Daisy asked bluntly.

Zoe nodded vigorously. "He's great and, newsflash, he's totally hot, and he likes her. A lot."

Zoe's comment sent my stomach into a tailspin. My heart felt funny. The problem was I liked Finn way too much. The intensity of my feelings had hurtled past anything I'd ever experienced before. I'd never have said I fell in love with Rick—better known as the cheating asshole—but it was hot and heavy and intense. My judgment had clouded the overall situation, and then the shame I felt when the truth came out had been crushing.

I didn't know what to think of what was happening with Finn. It was hot, it was heavy, it was intense, and it felt as if he'd slipped through the defenses around my heart. Which

I'd thought were airtight, to be honest. I didn't think he was anything like Rick, he wasn't that kind of man, but I didn't want my heart to get trampled on again. I had my pride. If I let myself think about it, I knew Finn meant far more to me than anyone had, which nearly sent me into a panic.

I looked around at my friends. All of them, despite their respective challenges, personal and otherwise, had found love. I hadn't thought love was in the cards for me. It felt like it required too much of a sacrifice. I didn't want to feel that vulnerable ever again.

So I lied through my teeth. "Maybe he likes me, but I'm not sure what I want yet. I'm not sure something serious is in the cards for me."

I felt Zoe's eyes on me and glanced her way. I could see the understanding in her gaze, and it made my throat tight. When I looked away, my eyes caught Harper's. If anyone understood vulnerability, she did.

I armored myself with my breezy attitude. "Oh Finn's hot. Don't get me wrong. I'm not saying I'm not going to enjoy what's happening, but for now I'm not thinking past it," I said bluntly.

Conveniently, our waiter arrived at that moment. I ordered another martini and breathed a sigh of relief that our conversation got knocked off track.

Later that night, I let myself into my apartment. Smokey looked up from the back of the couch when I clicked on the light. He started purring instantly before I even walked across the room, apparently in a friendly mood. I hung my jacket by the door and slipped off my shoes. Dropping my keys in the small bowl on the table by the door, the sound echoed in my apartment. I walked over to Smokey, curling my knuckles and stroking under his chin. His purring picked up speed as he leaned into my touch.

Most nights like this when I had dinner with friends, I would come home and unwind in front of the television. Rather than feeling relaxed after a dose of my girlfriends, I felt restless and prickly inside my skin. Probably because I lied to them all and acted as if Finn didn't mean nearly as much to me as he did. I didn't know why I lied. I needed to find a way to break things off with Finn because I didn't like how vulnerable I felt. Not one bit.

Chapter Twenty-Three

FINN

I leaned against the counter in my kitchen, running a hand through my hair as I waited for the coffee to finish brewing. It was early, and we had another court hearing today. Sutton's lawyers had engaged in a common delaying tactic used by those on the defense in court cases and asked for a continuance two days ago. I wouldn't have been surprised if they asked for another continuance today. The funny thing about the American legal system, touted for its fairness and its innocent until proven guilty proclamation was that defendants had far more tools at their disposal to slow the wheels of justice. Victims had few and often had to wait years for justice. Delaying tactics could make victims tired and weary, and it could reach a point where they would rather just drop everything than keep dealing with the process. The right to a speedy trial was for the defendant, not the accuser.

Jana filtered into my thoughts. Lately, she almost always danced at the edges, but the last few days she'd been remarkably quiet. I had heard little from her via text and was starting to wonder how she was doing. That was unusual for me. Even when I was seeing someone casually, I didn't banter back-and-forth. Texting wasn't quite my thing, but Jana's messages were funny and lighthearted. I hadn't realized I looked forward to them until she wasn't sending them. The past few days had been radio silence.

In an unusual move for me, I spun my phone around on the counter and quickly texted her. Tomorrow was Friday, and it would be good to see her again.

Dinner tomorrow?

The coffeemaker beeped. I poured a cup of coffee and walked to the windows, looking out over the misty morning in Seattle. Puget Sound was calm under the overcast sky. The slate gray sky blended into the steel gray of the ocean. Here and there, the sun shot through the clouds, casting glimmers of light on the ocean's surface.

Later that afternoon, after a crazy morning between the media and the hearing, I was starting to get worried. Jana had yet to reply to my text. I pulled it up again, not even thinking about the fact I was texting her again.

?

Brevity might've been a strong suit of mine.

An hour later, after dealing with a minor traffic accident, my phone vibrated on my desk. I spun it around to see Jana's reply.

I'm busy this weekend. I'll be out of town.

That was it. Something felt off. It was flat, as if she were canceling a business meeting with me. I sensed something was afoot with her. Yet, we were nothing more than what we were to each other. At least on the surface. I wanted to say something, to demand she give me more than that, but I didn't. If you wanted to know why, I wouldn't have been able to tell you. She'd rattled me.

I woke the following morning to the incessant buzzing of my

cell phone. I rubbed a hand over my face and reached drowsily to the table by my bed. "Fuck!"

I sat up, glancing around to find my phone. It was across the room on top of the dresser. Rolling out of bed, I sleepily trudged over and snagged it.

"Yes?" I asked, my voice gravelly from sleep.

"Finn?"

I gave my head a shake, confused to hear the sound of my little sister's voice.

"Sarah? What the hell are you calling at..." I paused to glance at the clock by my bed. The blue numbers read 6:00 AM.

"Sorry, Finn. I'm calling, well... I'm fine, but I got in a car accident with Remy..."

I was jolted out of my sleepy state. "Bloody hell, Sarah! Are you..."

"Calm down, Finn. I already said I was fine."

Sarah quickly explained. She and Remy, her current roommate and friend from university, had been driving from DC to Seattle for the holidays. Sarah thought nothing of the fact she hadn't bothered to share her plans with me, or our parents. Without a doubt, she was the free spirit in our family. Given my own life changing car accident years earlier, it took considerable effort not to lose my cool over this. Sarah assured me hurriedly that she was okay, but she had a broken ankle and a few bruises. The other issue was the car in question was totaled. I didn't like to consider what it meant the vehicle was totaled, but I forced my attention to the moment. Those questions could wait.

Within a few hours, I was on a plane out to meet Sarah in Bozeman, Montana. As the crow flew, it was a few hours away. I met Sarah and Remy at the hotel where they were staying. Sarah came barreling out of the room, swinging her arms around me.

"You came!"

She wobbled as she stepped away. "Easy with that ankle," I said as I steadied her.

"Oh, it's fine. It's just a crack," she offered.

"How did you manage nothing but a cracked ankle bone and yet the car is totaled?" I asked in return, scanning her.

Sarah looked perfectly fine with the exception of the removable air boot on her ankle. Her dark hair was pulled up into a ponytail, her blue eyes were bright, and she looked as easy going as ever.

She tugged me through the door into their hotel room.

Remy Simpson, Sarah's friend whom she'd met in university at Cambridge, grinned when she saw me. She was seated at a small round table in the room. She looked up from her laptop, brushing her blonde hair away from her face.

"We're fine, Finn. My car was kind of a beater. It's drivable, but my insurance company says it's totaled value-wise," Remy offered as she waved in my direction. "So I gotta get a new car."

I looked between the two of them as Sarah plunked down on the end of one of the beds.

"What's the plan?" I asked.

Sarah caught my eyes. "I don't know. You want to drive the rest of the way?"

"To Seattle?" I countered.

Sarah nodded, rather enthusiastically.

I shook my head. "I don't have time for a slow drive back, not to mention it's almost winter and there's snow on the ground. Driving through the mountains between here and Seattle won't exactly be fun."

Sarah sighed. With her rosy cheeks and her youthful, fresh faced look, her carefree spirit suited her. As soon as she'd graduated from university, she had bolted to the States.

"I can rent you two a car if you need."

Sarah swung her uninjured foot back and forth. "Nah. If I'm being realistic, my ankle's a little sore. I can't prop it up very easily in a car."

Remy chuckled, her brown eyes crinkling at the corners. "No, probably not."

"Okay, I'll take care of the tickets. You two can crash at my place in Seattle until you figure out what's next. Were you planning to let me know you were visiting?" I asked, my tone droll.

Sarah stood and threw her arms around me. "Yes!" She hopped back on her good foot. "I did text and say we might be coming for Christmas."

"So you did," I said wryly.

Sarah would consider a vague text of potential plans sufficient. I was used to this side of her, so I shrugged and moved on. I booked a room for the night at the same hotel and hopped online to purchase tickets to Seattle for all three of us. That night, I looked down at my phone, wondering if I should let Jana know I was out of town. I missed her. With the knowledge that Sarah was fine, I imagined it would've been fun to have Jana along with me on this unexpected trip.

Yet, I didn't let her know anything. I figured if she cared to know where I was, she'd make some effort to be in touch with me. That night over dinner and drinks with Sarah and her friend, I got the latest update on Sarah's new plan.

"I'm going back to London," she announced.

"Oh?"

Remy grinned. "She's in looove."

"Oh really?" I asked.

Sarah's cheeks got red, and she threw a glare at Remy. "I'm not in love." Glancing back to me, she continued. "You remember Colin," she said, referencing a guy she'd once dated in university.

"I do. He was nice enough," I replied, thinking that was about all I could recall of him.

"Thank God," Sarah said, gesturing at me with her straw. "Can you say something more enthusiastic?"

"What shall I say?" I countered wryly.

Remy cut in. "Your brother's not gonna think he's a hottie like you do."

Sarah's cheeks got redder. I remembered Colin. He *was* a nice chap. He'd been kind enough to help Sarah move flats several times during university and never once complained about it.

"I'm trying to recall if I met anyone else you dated, but I'm coming up blank. You brought him home to meet mom and dad. That's a good sign," I offered.

Sarah rolled her eyes. "Whatever. It's time for me to go back anyway. As much as it's fun to be here, I need to have a more stable job."

Sarah had bounced around traveling and picking up waitressing jobs here and there.

"Will you work for Dad?"

Sarah was a math genius actually, and her brilliance with numbers had our father nagging her periodically to work in his investment firm.

She cocked her head to the side and shrugged. "I probably should. Numbers are my thing."

Remy chuckled. "You should. You love anything to do with numbers. I can't say that for many people."

Conversation carried on as we caught up. Along the way, Sarah asked me, "So what are you doing? Why don't you go home and work for dad? You know you could."

"I know. Unlike you, it's not what I really want to do."

She held my gaze for a long moment. "Well then, what would you want to do? You have funds to invest. You don't need to be working your arse off as a cop."

Sarah had a point. I occasionally contemplated how I'd slid into my current position. With the aftershocks of my car accident, my plans to play professionally over, and then my blown up engagement, I'd needed something that mattered to me. So I'd become a police officer. My work mattered, and it had helped get me through the depressing years of letting go of another dream. I supposed it had been easier to swallow knowing I could someday walk away if I chose. Frankly, I could've walked away sooner and joined my father's investment firm, but I had absolutely zero interest in it.

The recent case with Sutton actually had me contemplating. I could sink my teeth into investments and raising money for projects that might make a difference. Changes in the court process for DV victims would be one project.

Somewhere along the way as dinner progressed, Sarah looked over at me with a sigh. She was slightly tipsy at this point. "So are you seeing anyone?"

Jana flashed through my thoughts, but I didn't know what to say about her. My hesitation was just long enough to cue Sarah. "Something's up."

I shook my head slightly. "Nah. I've gone on a few dates with someone recently, but that's it."

"What's her name?" Sarah asked, undeterred by my vague reply.

"Jana," I said succinctly.

"Is it serious?"

Bloody hell. I occasionally forgot how persistent Sarah could be.

"I wouldn't say so."

"It's time for you to move on," she declared. "Right Remy?"

Remy had enough sense to stay out of this one and simply shrugged, pulling up her phone and scrolling through something on the screen.

"Move on from what?" I asked.

"From Kristen."

"Sarah, I'm not hung up on Kristen. I haven't been for years. Speaking of Kristen, she told me she talked to you. She was all put out I didn't tell her about my trust fund. Mind letting me know next time you decide to gab to my ex?" I asked before taking a drag from my beer.

Sarah rolled her eyes. "She called me! I was just trying to get on her nerves. I guess it worked, huh?"

At my eye roll, she continued, "Anyway, you haven't dated anyone in forever."

"Bloody hell, Sarah. I've dated."

She cocked her head to the side and glared at me. "No you haven't."

"Sarah, I'm not celibate if that's what you're worried about."

"Gah! I don't want to hear about your sex life," she said quickly.

"Well then, stop being so nosy."

"Jana is the first woman's name you've even mentioned. Tell me about her," she demanded.

Remy burst out laughing, finally interrupting. "You are probably the single most annoying little sister ever!"

Sarah swatted her on the shoulder. "I am not!"

I chuckled. "Remy might have a point. Anyway, I've seen Jana a few times and I like her, but that's about all there is to tell."

My heart gave a hard thump. *Like* didn't quite capture how I felt about Jana, and I bloody well knew it. Yet, I didn't like thinking about it, not if she was going to create distance like she had. Another voice inside me kept reminding me that Jana had her own baggage and trust was a bit of a challenge for her. I sensed she'd gotten skittish. But I bloody hell didn't know what to do about it.

Chapter Twenty-Four

FINN

I woke early the following morning to the buzz of my phone vibrating on the night table. I fumbled for it, and saw Becca's name flash on the screen. I quickly answered, sliding up against the headboard in my hotel bed.

"Becca, what's up?"

"Did I wake you up?" she asked.

"In case you missed it, it's Saturday," I offered sarcastically.

"Right," she replied without a hint of laughter. "Thought you'd want to know Ray Sutton is playing games with his no-contact order. He was spotted visiting a supposed friend in the same condominium complex where Lynne Sutton is staying with her family."

I rubbed the sleep out of my eyes. "I'm only surprised because I'd think he want to keep as low a profile as possible with the election coming up soon," I replied, sliding up against the pillows. "I'm assuming there's nothing we can do about it."

"I plan to bring it up at our next hearing. I thought you'd want to know just to make sure your unit is up to speed if he pushes the limits too far. Do you have any units patrolling that area?" Becca asked.

"Of course. Not just my unit, but any of them assigned know to circle through that complex. I'll touch base with Eli and have him follow up with the weekend guys. I'm not on duty this weekend."

"Since when did that keep you from working?" Becca asked wryly.

I kicked the sheets off and swung my legs off the bed, glancing at the digital clock by the bed. It read 7:00am. "I'm actually in Montana, so I'm definitely not working."

"What are you doing in Montana?" Becca asked.

I quickly explained the situation with Sarah. "I'll be back in Seattle by this evening."

"Oh, another thing," Becca added. "I ran into Zoe Walsh yesterday, and she said Ray came by trying to persuade her to take his case again. Thank God she turned him down."

"Why would he be scouting around? He already has an attorney."

"Because Zoe's one of the best, and he wants her," Becca said flatly.

I didn't like thinking Ray was anywhere near Jana, no matter how irrational it seemed. "Mind doing me a favor?"

"Of course," Becca said swiftly.

"Ask Aidan to have his guys keep an eye on Zoe's office building," I said. Aidan ran one of the premier security companies in Seattle. If anyone could make sure Ray didn't pull anything slick, it would be Aidan and his team.

"I'm sure it won't be a problem, but..." She paused and then laughed softly. "You're worried about Jana, aren't you?"

I stood from the bed and strode toward the hotel windows, pushing back the curtains to discover it had snowed during the night. The mountains surrounding Bozeman were dusted with white. "Nothing big. Just think it's worth keeping an eye on Ray wherever he might go."

"You think he would do something with this much atten-tion on him?"

"I don't know what he would do, but desperate men do desperate things."

After Becca hung up, I held my phone in my hand. Before I let myself think about it, I called Jana.

She answered on the first ring. As soon as she spoke, it occurred to me it was mere minutes past 7:00am, and I had no good reason to call other than that I was thinking about her.

"Hello?" she repeated when I didn't immediately reply.

"Jana, it's Finn," I said.

"Finn?" she asked, her voice husky with sleep.

"I probably woke you up," I said rather belatedly.

There was a long pause, and I heard a rustling sound. I imagined her warm and sleepy and wished I was there with her.

"You did, but that's okay. My alarm went off a bit ago. What are you calling about?"

I couldn't say I was thinking too clearly. "Oh, Becca McNamara called to update me on a few things and mentioned in passing Ray Sutton tried to persuade Zoe to take his case again. Since he's nosing around, I asked her to have Aidan's guys check the building periodically."

"Oh. My. God. That's ridiculous," Jana snapped.

Maybe it was, maybe it wasn't. Just now, I was tired, and I missed Jana. I definitely wasn't thinking clearly. I didn't bloody fucking care if she was upset about it.

"I did. It's just a precaution. I'll check on things when I'm back..."

"Where are you?" she asked, cutting in.

For the first time, I heard a hint of worry in her voice. I quickly explained, adding at the end, "Long story short, I came to get my sister and her friend. We're flying back to Seattle this afternoon. I'll be there this evening."

"Oh," Jana said, her tone shifting from concerned to controlled.

"I thought you were out of town," I commented.

She was quiet for a beat. "Change of plans," she finally said.

"Can I stop by tonight?"

She went quiet again. Her sigh filtered through the phone. "I don't know if that's a good idea, Finn. I'm not sure what we're doing. Maybe we should take a step back."

I didn't know what we were either, but here in this moment of missing her, I knew she was more than just a passing fling. Yet, I didn't know how to have this conversation over the phone while I was close to a thousand miles away. So I took a breath and shackled my words.

"I'll call you when I land. If anything comes up, please let me know."

"I will," she said softly.

There was so much more I wanted to say, but I said nothing.

Chapter Twenty-Five

JANA

Even though it was Saturday, I went into the office that afternoon because there was always something I could do. I'd been restless ever since I'd spoken to Finn this morning. I felt like I was tilting through my day, dizzy from my own internal state. I needed to take a step back. I didn't trust myself to navigate the intimacy I felt with him. I couldn't say why, but I didn't believe I could have something like that. I was annoyed Finn had asked Aidan's security company to check on our office building. There was nothing to worry about. Yet, it felt good to know he was concerned for me. That feeling was a curl of warmth around my heart. Though I didn't want to savor it so much, I did.

I let myself in the quiet office, locking the door behind me and settling down to get to work on some court filings. Hours later, the doorknob rattled at the front and my heart flew into my chest. Then, I heard a key slide into the lock and knew it must be Zoe. She stepped inside, closing the door behind her, her eyes widening when she turned to see me at the desk.

"What are you doing here?" she asked.

"Working," I offered with a shrug, feigning a casual tone. "What are you doing here?"

"Same actually. I stopped by to grab my laptop." She stared at me for a moment, her gaze assessing. "Are you okay?"

"Yeah. I'm fine. Are you?"

"Yup. I'm fine. Are you and Finn doing anything this weekend?" she asked.

I shook my head quickly. "Nope. We're not like a *thing*," I explained, my tone more defensive than I wished.

Zoe stepped from the door and slipped into the chair across from my desk. "Are you doing that thing where you're pushing him away?" she asked bluntly.

"What are you talking about?" I asked.

She brushed her hair back away from her face, tucking it behind her ears. She had glorious hair, rich auburn flecked with gold. I felt silly in comparison with my brown hair and wild purple streaks.

"You've done this before," she said pointedly.

"Done what?" I countered, fighting the defensiveness rising inside.

"Okay, I know the thing with Rick was a mess. It was embarrassing, and I know you were ashamed of how it played out. I totally get that. But..." She paused for a beat, looking torn. My gut churned, but I waited it out.

"I can see why you ended up getting involved with Rick," she finally said.

My heart twisted in my chest. Hurt, I stared at her, tears pressing at the backs of my eyes. "What do you mean?"

"Look," she said softly "We've been friends since college. I'm not a therapist, but if I had to guess, I would say that because of the way things happened with your dad..."

I cut in. "Nothing happened with my dad. He was *never* around," I said, my tone downright sullen now.

Undeterred, Zoe continued, "Exactly. He left you and your mom right after you were born. You're like the super-independent woman. That's how I think of you. Always standing on your own, ready to take on the world. I love that about you. I totally respect it, and I get it. If that's what you want from life, that's what you should have. My point is, before Rick, when you were dating in college and whatnot, you..." Her words trailed off, and she looked at me carefully.

I was listening intently even though my heart hurt, and it felt like Zoe was tearing open old scars.

"Well, you always backed off if anything got close to serious with someone. You didn't give things a chance to be more than casual. I'm not saying you should've gotten serious with anyone. Hell, I was still a virgin back in college, so it's not that. I'm just trying to say this thing it seems like you're doing is what you usually did."

My chest felt tight, and my throat was clogged. I swallowed, beating back the tears. "Uh-huh," I managed. "What does this have to do with why I might've been so blind about Rick?"

I hated how stupid I felt about him. I couldn't untangle whether my shame was because it turned into a public humiliation, or due to how bad I felt about unintentionally being part of someone else's pain and betrayal.

Zoe chewed on her bottom lip and sighed. "The whole 'fling with your boss' is a fantasy for lots of people. It's hot and off limits. No matter what I think of Rick, he's definitely handsome." I rolled my eyes, and she laughed softly. "Anyway, since it's off limits, it's sort of a failsafe that it probably won't get serious. It's not like you were in love with Rick. The way it played out just reinforced what you already thought, which is you shouldn't assume anybody will be there for you," she said carefully.

Zoe was hitting so close to home, the pain stung. I didn't realize a tear rolled down my cheek until she leaned forward and nudged the tissues on the corner of my desk in my direction. Another tear fell, and I grabbed a tissue, quickly wiping at my eyes.

"I don't know why I'm crying. I'm sorry."

"For God's sake, don't apologize for crying. You're my best friend and you didn't hesitate to tell me the truth when I needed to hear it. When I buried myself at work and got accidentally too uptight about Ethan, you pushed me to get over myself and give him a chance. He was the best decision I ever made besides you being my best friend," she said fiercely, her own eyes bright with tears. "I'm not saying you should be with somebody, but let it be because it's an actual choice, not just because you're scared. Finn seems like a great guy. I think he really likes you, and it's pretty obvious you really like him."

Another tear rolled down my cheek. I swiped it with the balled up tissue. "I don't know what I want, and I don't know what he wants," I muttered.

"I know it's not easy. There's no guarantee, but come on, Jana. What would you say if our situations were reversed?"

I thought about Finn, and the way he looked at me when we were tangled up together. I thought about how funny and gracious he was. I thought about our phone call this morning. I knew with certainty if a man like him was interested in my best friend—minus the detail she was already head over heels in love with Ethan—I would tell her to give him a chance.

I finally met her eyes again and sighed. "I'll try to think about it."

"You'll *try* to think about it?" she asked with a little laugh.

"Yes. I'll try. Old habits die hard. Maybe you're right, maybe I don't really have faith anybody will be there for me because that's what life's shown me. I just... I just need to figure it out at my own pace."

"Okay," she said softly. "You get right on trying to think about thinking about it," she said with a wry grin.

We laughed together, and I glanced up at the clock above the door. "It's almost five, what are you doing tonight?"

"How about we grab a few drinks together before I go home and work?"

I blew my nose and glanced over. "You don't have plans with Ethan?"

"He's helping Liam with some bathroom remodeling project. He won't be home until later."

In short order, we were ensconced at a table in the corner at Harry's, a basic pub where we could have some privacy and enjoy people watching. We ordered some appetizers and nibbled on them as we enjoyed a few beers. After our heavy conversation at the office, we hewed to easy topics, such as whether the Seattle Stars would have a good season. Zoe was the best kind of friend. She would call me out on stuff, as I would with her, and then she would leave it be.

She commiserated with me when I recounted the remaining three courses I needed to complete to graduate from law school. "That last semester sucked," she said bluntly.

"I know. I kinda blanked out because my mom was sick. I was too overwhelmed, but I can't help but wonder if I could've gotten through it if it hadn't been such heavy courses."

"I don't know. Even though I didn't have anything like that going on, I got through by the skin of my teeth."

"You graduated summa cum laude," I said with a roll of my eyes.

She returned my eye roll. "Right, but it was a ton of work. Don't forget you had straight A's too. Don't act like I'm something special. You were always the smartest one in every class we had together."

I shrugged. School had been something I did well. I hated that I had to put on hold finishing it, but now that I'd finally re-enrolled at Zoe's nudging, I was relieved. No matter what I did, I wanted to finish what I started. Conversation moved along with Zoe sharing her worries about when to have kids. "I just don't know about the timing. I'm trying to imagine my life right now and adding a baby," she said, her eyes wide before she took a long drag from her beer.

I laughed. "I get it. A whole human, and you're totally responsible for them."

"Exactly, that's what I'm freaking out about."

"Okay, I get the concern, but you work for yourself. I'm not saying it won't be hard. But, you can set your own schedule. It's a lot to think about. I've never been one of those people who knew right off I wanted to have kids."

Zoe nodded. "Me neither, but I'm pretty sure I do now."

My heart gave a little squeeze. There was a time when I was younger that I'd been all about having kids, but I never quite believed it would happen for me. I'd shut those thoughts away.

"What about Ethan?"

"Oh he's great. He teases because that's what he does about everything, but he says he'll wait until I'm ready and if I'm never ready, he's fine with that too. I think it would make him sad, but he would be okay."

I flashed a grin. "He's a good egg. I'm glad I nagged you into him."

Zoe's cheeks flushed. "Oh I was a goner at the start, but without you, I might've chickened out."

Her comment struck right at the heart of what she'd been trying to tell me earlier. I shook those thoughts away. I needed a respite from my messy emotions.

A fresh basket of chips arrived. The interruption knocked us off that topic. As I nibbled on a chip, Zoe commented, "2 o'clock."

"What?" I asked, confused.

"Your 2 o'clock. Finn's ex is at that table."

"Oh!"

I caught myself about to look rather obviously in that direction.

"Don't make it too obvious," she said with a giggle.

"Right." I carefully slid my gaze in that direction. There was a table with two women and a man. "Which one?"

"The blonde one."

"Are you sure?"

Zoe nodded firmly. I studied the woman. She was slender with long blonde hair and fine boned, classic features. She conveniently stood to walk up to the bar and ask for something from the bartender. She wore black slacks, a white blouse and low heels. Totally boring if you asked me. I looked back to Zoe.

"Bland much?" I asked rhetorically.

The moment I spoke, I felt bad. I didn't like that Finn elicited irrational jealousy in me, nor did I like to be that woman who bashed other women.

Zoe snorted. "Be nice."

"I know. I shouldn't have said that. It was my insecurity talking," I said sheepishly. "She's gorgeous and classy. I'm not."

"Oh shut up. You're fucking gorgeous," Zoe said bluntly. "Everywhere I go with you, men are drooling. You've got a hot body and gorgeous hair. So maybe she's beautiful in her own way, but trust me, you stand out."

I shrugged. Accepting compliments had never come easily for me. "If that's the woman Finn wanted to marry, I'm totally not his type."

Zoe sighed elaborately. "That's the direction you're going with this? I can't believe I said anything."

"Why did you?" I asked, feeling suddenly quite insecure about who I was and how I looked, all because I saw Finn's ex.

"I just noticed her and was curious. That's all. I suppose it's proven one thing."

"Huh?"

"You're jealous," she retorted, a gleam in her eyes.

What I didn't say aloud was I now had three things bothering me. I was having a hard time believing I could have a shot with Finn. I got anxious just thinking about the depth of my feelings for him. Now, I saw the woman he had once asked to marry him, and she was nothing like me—perfect, blonde and proper. I seriously doubted she'd ever been stupid enough to have a flaming affair with her boss who turned out to be married. Only I could pull that off. On top of it all, I couldn't believe I was jealous and what it meant.

Chapter Twenty-Six

FINN

A few days after I returned with Sarah and Remy, I sat at the kitchen counter, watching while Sarah made omelets for us. Having the two of them here was a sad reminder of how lonely my life usually was. I didn't think much about it. I buried myself in work and carried on, only occasionally considering whether I wanted to make a change. Aside from one brief call with Jana, I hadn't spoken to her since I'd returned. To say she was giving off stay-away vibes was an understatement. It didn't change the fact I missed her.

I snagged my cup of coffee and strode to stand at the windows and make a quick call while Remy and Sarah chatted. Eli answered on the first ring. "What's up?"

"Just checking on our coverage schedule for next week. Any updates?"

"Not since I talked to you the day before yesterday," Eli replied with a laugh. "You okay? You sound, I dunno, maybe not so great."

"Oh, I'm fine. With my sister here, I've got a few things to work around. That's all."

On its face, my answer was entirely true. In fact, I'd

rearranged most of my work schedule for the next few weeks to have time to visit with Sarah over the holidays. Yet, I was pointlessly calling Eli about something that could definitely wait until later.

"Why don't you call her?" Eli asked bluntly.

I'd shared a bit about how Jana had stalled me the other day over coffee with him. It spoke volumes that Jana was getting to me enough I mentioned it to anyone.

I wished I could laugh about his question, but I hated the fact Jana was pretty much not talking to me right now.

"Waiting for the right time," was all I said.

We said our goodbyes and ended the call. I stared at my phone, contemplating a call to Jana. I sensed I needed to give her some space. Hell, she'd flat told me we needed to take a step back. But I missed her. With Sarah and Remy here for however long, they figured into any plans I made, so I supposed it was best for now.

The following day, I was at the station for a few meetings and to take care of some paperwork. It was mostly static for me, but the calls about Ray Sutton's case seemed endless. Between the media and Sutton's attorney, it was something almost every day. His attorney was pushing hard for Becca to drop down to lesser charges, but she wasn't biting. I was bloody glad Becca had the case because she didn't back down easy.

Later in the afternoon, I chatted with Eli when he popped in my office to catch up. After a rather normal conversation, he asked, "So you seeing Jana again?"

I shifted my shoulders and sighed, spinning my empty coffee cup in a circle on my desk before restlessly standing and filling it again. "Not at the moment." I didn't add that I'd left her two messages over the last few days, and she hadn't called me back.

Eli stood when his cell phone rang. "Gotta grab this, but seems to me like you might want to call her," he said with a laugh.

Eli's comments were teasing and casual, yet he couldn't know they were barbs to me. The ache from missing Jana was acute. Calling her clearly wasn't changing a damn thing.

———

Another few days passed uneventfully, and then I had a cryptic message from Zoe Walsh. I didn't have a single case right now with her, so it didn't make sense for her to call me. I returned her call immediately.

"Hi Zoe. You called?"

"Finn! Hello. I did call," she said before pausing.

"I didn't think you were handling any cases I was working on. Has that changed?"

Zoe's sigh filtered through the phone. "This might seem weird, but I'm calling about Jana."

"Is she okay?" I asked quickly, worry flashing through me.

"She's fine. She's, well, she's cranky," Zoe finally said.

Puzzled, I was quiet for a moment before I spoke. "Uh, okay. What shall I do about that? She hasn't really been in touch. The last time we spoke, she said she thought it would be better if we took a step back."

"If I say too much, Jana will get pissed and she's my best friend," Zoe explained.

"I respect that. A few clues would be helpful," I said.

"Okay, here goes. I don't know you that well, but Ethan says you're a good guy, and I just have a feeling about you two. I don't usually butt in like this, but I have to ask. How much do you like Jana?"

Bloody hell. I couldn't believe she was asking me this. I missed Jana like crazy. Hell, I'd asked Kristen to marry me, and my feelings hadn't run nearly as deep as they did with Jana. I adored her—her quirky, bold personality, her silliness, her wild hair, her lush body, and her big heart.

"A lot," I finally said.

Zoe was quiet long enough that I started to feel foolish.

She finally spoke. "She likes you a lot too. She's been a real pain in the ass about it. It's not my place to get into why, but you might need to go out of your way to make your point with her."

"Go out of my way?"

"Yeah, she doesn't realize how awesome she is. She's worth it, Finn. She's one of the best people I know," Zoe said, so earnestly it made my heart ache.

My throat tightened and my heart knocked against my ribs. "I know," I said quietly. And I did know. I'd never met anyone like her. The way she'd shimmied through my defenses straight to my heart was almost shocking to me. Perhaps that's what had left me stuck spinning my wheels ever since she'd said she wanted to take a step back.

There was a long silence. I realized Zoe wasn't going to add anymore, and I didn't know what else to say. In an effort to lighten the moment, I asked, "How she's dealing with the security checks?"

Zoe chuckled. "Actually she was bitching about it the other day, but it's fine. They only come by once a day."

"Glad to hear she's bitching about it. I'd be worried if she wasn't," I said with a chuckle.

"So true," Zoe replied.

After I got off the call with Zoe, I contemplated just what the hell she meant. I couldn't deny the depth of my feelings for Jana. The word love feathered along the edges of my mind.

Chapter Twenty-Seven

JANA

Another weekend passed, and I was cranky as hell. I missed Finn, and I didn't know what the hell to do about missing him. Somehow the fact it was so close to Christmas made everything worse. The cheery holiday lights made me miss my mom and wish I had someone to share the holidays with. Usually, this wasn't an issue for me. I celebrated with my friends and visited Sal and June. Now, all I did was think about Finn. I kept replaying my conversation with Zoe and contemplating her point that I had a pattern of not giving anyone a chance. I felt like a fool because I was the human equivalent of a dog chasing my tail—round and round in my mind, but I went nowhere.

I was fielding phone calls one afternoon when Zoe was at court, contemplating whether I should talk to her for advice. I was startled when Lynne Sutton stepped through the entrance. She closed the door quietly behind her and stepped to my desk. "How can I help you?" I asked.

"I had a message from my attorney asking me to meet him here," she finally explained, tucking her blonde hair behind her ears. She looked nervous, and I was suddenly anxious because I knew there was no such meeting.

I managed our schedule. It also didn't make sense for Lynne to come here at her attorney's behest. I hoped I was wrong, though my gut told me I wasn't. Something was off.

"Let me check on this for you," I said with a forced smile.

I quickly called Zoe. "Hi there, did you have a meeting this afternoon?" I asked right away.

"Huh?" Zoe asked, sounding rightly confused. "You know I have a hearing in an hour."

I did know that. "That's what I thought. I have Lynne Sutton here, saying that we have a meeting with her attorney."

"Something's up. We have no such meeting," Zoe said quickly.

"I understand," I said smoothly, my thoughts racing through who would have sent Lynne here and why.

"I'm getting off this call and calling the security team. Ray Sutton's up to something," she said quickly.

"Right. You do that. What should I tell her?"

"Be honest, but don't let her leave. We'll figure it out."

The line went dead, and I looked over at Lynne. My stomach churned.

"Ms. Sutton..."

"Call me Lynne," she interjected.

"Lynne, no meeting was ever scheduled. I don't believe that message came from your attorney, and we're concerned your ex is up to something," I said quickly.

Lynne's eyes widened. "Oh my God. Should I..."

"Don't leave," I said in anticipation of her question.

I stood and rounded the desk, locking the door behind us.

I sat down in the chair at an angle across from her. Her hands were shaking, and my gut churned away while my pulse raced, anxiety chewing me up inside.

The phone rang. I reached over and answered from where I sat. It was Zoe.

"Aidan's sending a team over from the courthouse. I called Finn too," she said.

"That's not..."

"I know you're avoiding him, but it's ridiculous. He's already on his way."

Tears pricked at the back of my eyes, and my throat tightened. I couldn't really focus on my feelings for him, but everything had been bubbling under the surface for too long. I forced myself to be rational. "Okay thanks."

There was a loud banging on the door. "Gotta go," I said, hanging up quickly.

"Lynne, I know you're in there," a man's voice called.

I certainly didn't know Ray Sutton well, but he'd been on enough political ads lately for me to recognize his voice.

"Oh no," Lynne said, twisting her hands together.

"Security's on the way over here," I said swiftly. The banging continued.

I looked to Lynne. "Just wait. The police are on the way too."

We waited for what felt like forever, but I knew it was mere minutes before we heard someone else approaching in the hall. The banging stopped. Lynne was frozen where she was in her chair. Much as I wanted to open the door to find out what was going on, I wanted her to feel safe, so I glued my ear to the door and listened. I heard a low voice telling Ray to calm down and asking him why he was there.

I looked back to Lynne and spoke. "It's okay, the security guard's talking to him."

She looked back at me, her eyes wide. "I'm sure you think I'm crazy, but..."

"I know you're not crazy," I said firmly.

I leaned close to the door again and heard Finn's voice telling Ray he was in violation of the no contact order.

Ray started to argue. "What are you talking about? Lynne isn't here..."

I didn't think anymore and swung the door open, stepping outside and yanking it closed behind me. Finn, the security guy, and Ray all turned toward me. "You were just banging on the door calling her name. You knew Lynne was in there," I said bluntly.

The relief I felt at seeing Finn was so profound, my knees went wobbly. I wanted to leap into his arm, but now was definitely not the time. His eyes caught mine, something flickering in them, but he kept his attention on Ray. Another officer approached from the hallway, speaking into his radio.

The process of arresting Ray began. Zoe also returned, reporting she'd asked to reschedule her court hearing. Within a few minutes, the hallway was bustling. Finn caught my eyes and stepped to my side. "Okay if I speak to Lynne in the office?" he asked, his voice low.

"Of course," I said, nodding quickly.

His hand rested briefly on my back. Just that simple touch, and I wanted to cry. My emotions were a cacophony inside.

I needed to get a grip. I gave myself a shake and let Finn into the office, stepping inside behind him. Lynne was sitting exactly where I left her. She wasn't crying. She was quite still, her face was pale and her eyes were wide. Her hands were clasped together in her lap as if holding onto herself for comfort. Finn approached her and sat in the chair beside her, quickly checking in and explaining that Ray had been arrested for violating the no contact order.

I knew he needed to do what he needed to do right now, but I desperately wanted to talk to him.

You don't even know what you want to say. Or maybe you do. Better figure it out first.

I swatted my thoughts away and tried to stay out of everyone's way. I gave an official interview to Finn's partner when he directed me to talk with him. Finn pulled me aside before he left. I looked up into his eyes. Words were jammed up in my throat. I had so much to say, and yet I couldn't gather my thoughts into anything sensible.

"My sister and her friend are here for a bit staying with me. I don't suppose we could try to get dinner soon? Tonight's out because it'll be a shitshow at the station since Ray's a bloody mayoral candidate," he said.

I nodded, my throat tight. "Okay," I finally said.

We were standing behind my desk, just in front of the door that led into my small private office. It was all I could do not to yank him in there. I couldn't look away from his deep blue gaze. Despite the fact we had two police officers here, the security team and Lynne's attorney—who had confirmed she'd never scheduled a meeting with Zoe—it felt as if we were alone.

He finally nodded tightly and then left. Fuck, fuck, fuck. I needed to figure this out.

Chapter Twenty-Eight

FINN

I'd been pondering Zoe's comment that I needed to do something big to let Jana know how much she mattered. The idea came to me in a flash. After conferring with Eli, who thought I was plain crazy, but happy to go along with my plan, I set the wheels in motion. Later the following day with everything in place, including a little help from Zoe and Ethan, I headed out to respond to a fender bender in the middle of evening rush hour. I was breaking quite a few rules today, and I didn't give a bloody damn.

With my lights flashing, I eased onto the shoulder of the highway and climbed out of my car to find Jana standing with her arms crossed as she stared at the dented bumper and back to Eli. Ethan had readily agreed to sacrifice his bumper. Jana spun in my direction, her cheeks flushed and her brow furrowed. Eli had done beautifully with nothing more than a slight dent in Ethan's bumper.

Eli was leaning against his car, a gleam in his eyes, but he kept a straight face.

"Sorry Officer. This lady was going so damn slow, I bumped into her," he offered, thumbing in Jana's direction.

Jana already looked flustered, but now she looked pissed. She shot a glare at him and huffed before looking to me. "I had to slow down. I mean, it's busy here," she said, flinging a hand toward the slow rolling traffic.

Eli nodded along, playing the lazy-don't-give-a-damn part he'd decided upon perfectly. "You sure did slow down. If you hadn't done that, I wouldn't have bumped you. No worries. You got my insurance info." Ignoring Jana's huff and the fire shooting from her eyes, he looked my way and shrugged again. "No idea why she's so pissed. I'm taking the blame."

Jana crossed her arms and tapped her foot. Bloody hell. She looked beautiful. Her hair was down today, a loose tangle around her shoulders. Pink was mingling again with the purple streaks in her hair. She wore a stretchy black skirt that fell just above her knees with a fitted blue blouse. Bloody hell. I wanted her. My body was revving at the mere sight of her, and my heart ached.

I realized she was probably quite stressed because she was driving Ethan's car. I met her gaze. "Doesn't look too bad. Why don't you come chat with me in my patrol car about it?" I asked.

Her eyes widened, her arms falling open. "It wasn't my fault. Why do you need to talk to me?"

Eli sighed. "We're good. Already told her I'll pay for it even though she slammed on her brakes. I don't know why she's being so bitchy."

Jana stomped past him. "Fine. I'll be happy to talk to you if I don't have to listen to this idiot."

I rolled my eyes at Eli as we walked past, wondering if I'd pushed things a little too far here. I didn't particularly care if I did. I enjoyed the view of her lush ass as she stomped down the pavement to my car. After I situated her in the passenger seat and slid into the front beside her, I unhooked the cuffs from my belt, reached over and immediately cuffed her.

"What the hell are you doing?"

"Trying to talk to you," I said bluntly.

Her pulse fluttered wildly in her neck, her breath came out in a huff, and she stared at me. For a flash, her eyes narrowed and then she burst out laughing.

"Okay, okay," she managed after she stopped laughing.

"I also owe you these cuffs," I said.

Her gaze darkened, need flickered in the depths, the flush on her cheeks deepened, but she didn't look away. "That you do. Are you on duty officer?"

I shook my head.

"I can't leave right now. Zoe asked me to pick up Ethan's car, so I need to call him."

I wasn't good at keeping up the front because her eyes narrowed as I stared at her.

"You knew about this."

I failed completely and chuckled.

"Eli's a friend. I'm paying for Ethan's new bumper."

She started laughing so hard tears ran down her cheeks. When she stopped laughing, she bit her lip. "Well, you certainly got my attention."

I looked at her for a long moment, soaking in this wild, funny, bold woman who'd stolen my heart in record time. My heart thudded inside my chest. I swallowed against the emotion knotting inside and held her gaze, taking a deep breath. "Zoe suggested I might need to do something to get your attention, so I did. I don't know what I mean to you, but you..."

I hadn't thought through this part. With all of my planning, I hadn't considered what I meant to say.

My words just slipped out. "I think I'm falling in love with you, and I know it's crazy and..."

Jana's breath hitched loudly, and a tear rolled down her cheek. Suddenly, she was crawling across the console in between us into my lap and dusting kisses all over my face.

She drew back, her eyes glittering. "Me too. I feel crazy, and I'm sorry I shut you out and I just...."

She mumbled a bunch of stuff into my neck, most of which I couldn't understand. Because it was Jana and my body did what it did whenever she was close, I was hard inside of a second. She finally leaned back again, dragging her sleeve across her face with a sigh. Her eyes caught mine and darkened. The air around us was heavy, weighted with desire and longing. She settled her hips down, rolling over my cock. Unfortunately or fortunately, depending on how you looked at it, I could feel the damp heat of her through my uniform and her panties. Her skirt had ridden up around her hips, and there was nothing else between us.

There was a sharp knock on the window. I glanced over to see Eli and Ethan standing outside.

"We have company," I murmured, my voice gruff.

Unabashed, Jana shrugged. "Do I have to get off your lap?" she asked with a sly grin.

"Yeah, you do. At least for now."

"Do I get to keep these?" she asked, wiggling her hands in the cuffs.

"Sure," I said, my cock hardening just at the look in her eyes.

I opened the door after she climbed out of my lap with a reluctant sigh. Stepping out of the car, I glanced between Eli and Ethan. "Okay guys, we're all set, right?"

Ethan grinned. "So I get a new bumper and you get the girl, huh?"

"That's the plan," I said with a wink.

They said their goodbyes, and I climbed back in the car, driving off with Jana beside me. I meant to take her back to her place, but she was impatient. The handcuffs were no deterrent. Her hands were all over me. Instead of one palm on my cock as I tried to drive, she had two and blamed it on the fact her hands were cuffed together.

To say my driving was erratic was an understatement. It was late evening, and I turned off onto a road outside of Seattle to a usually empty cul-de-sac. It was a building project that had been abandoned back in the days of the housing boom. I drove swiftly down the gravel road, rolling to a stop in a deserted area amongst the trees.

I looked to her, leaning over and catching her lips in a kiss. She clambered over the console again, straddling me and looping her cuffed hands around my neck. Yet again, any attempt at orchestrating anything flew out the window. Her tongue tangled with mine, her hips rolled against me, and I tore at her blouse. I broke free from our kiss, gulping in air. Her breasts tumbled loose when I flicked the clasp between them. Her dusky pink nipples were taut against my thumbs. Dipping my head, I drew one into my mouth. I'd missed everything about her—the scent of her, the taste of her, how wild and unrestrained she was. She cried out, gasping when I bit down on her nipple.

I savored the lush weight of her breasts in my palms. Lifting my head, I found her eyes dark and intent.

"Unbutton your shirt," she ordered.

"I think you have it backwards," I said with a slow grin. "Aren't I supposed to be the one giving orders?"

She flashed a smile. "Maybe, but I can't unbutton your shirt, and I want to feel you, so get it done."

I was happy to oblige, swiftly unbuttoning my shirt and groaning when she shimmied closer, her breasts brushing against my chest. I slid my hands up her legs, savoring the flex of her muscles as she rolled her hips against me. The black silk between her thighs was wet.

I glanced down as I shoved her skirt up. She ground her hips against me. I rose up to meet her, savoring her rough cry. I pushed her back a little and teased my fingers across the drenched silk.

"I missed you," I murmured, looking back up to see her wide blue eyes darken. As I held her gaze, my heart pounding hard and fast, vulnerability flashed in her gaze.

I wanted her fiercely, more fiercely than I'd ever wanted anyone.

Chapter Twenty-Nine

JANA

Finn's gaze held mine, hot and dark. I was a tornado of emotion inside. I needed him inside of me. *Now.*

When he dragged his fingers across the damp silk between my thighs again, I rolled my hips restlessly against him. "Unbutton your pants," I ordered.

He chuckled again. "I think you still have this backwards."

"You can boss me around, but I'm better at it," I said with a laugh.

His mouth curled at one corner, sending my belly into a tailspin of flutters. I rose up as he reached between us, unbuttoning his pants swiftly. I glanced down to see the hard ridge of his cock outlined by his fitted black briefs. I sank down again, rubbing my wet pussy over his boxers. My panties were so wet, I knew he could feel it. His eyes darkened and his breath hissed through his teeth.

"Not enough. Get your briefs out of the way," I said.

His eyes locked to mine, I felt him reach between us, his knuckles brushing over my clit and sending a sharp spike of pleasure through me. I looked down to see his cock spring free of his briefs. Shifting them down, he gripped his cock in his fist and shoved my panties out of the way, dragging his fingers through my slick folds. Teasing me again, he sank a finger knuckle deep inside me, another finger swiftly joining it. I cried out. I was slippery wet, frantic for more.

"More," I gasped, rolling my hips into his touch as he pumped his fingers in and out of me.

I shimmied closer, sighing at the feel of his hard, hot muscled chest against my breasts. On a groan, he slipped his fingers out and positioned his cock at my entrance, dragging the thick head of it back and forth, teasing over my clit and soaking his cock in my juices.

"Finn," I gasped, his name a plea.

With our gazes locked, I sank down over his cock as he thrust up into me. I cried out at the delicious stretch. Having Finn buried inside of me was like coming home. I held still, emotion rocking me. My blouse had slipped off my shoulders and hung around my waist. He stroked his palm down my spine, and I savored the warm strength in his touch as he pulled me closer and began to rock into me. We didn't have much room to maneuver. The steering wheel rubbed against my low back as we began to move.

It was the hottest sex I'd ever had in my life.

We moved in slow motion. It felt like my orgasm teetered on the edge forever, waves of pleasure spiraling through me with every roll of his hips. In our compressed position, my clit rubbed against him. I rocked into him, wanting him deeper and deeper with every roll. Leaning forward, I nipped my teeth along his neck.

"I want to see you," he muttered gruffly.

I lifted my head as Finn gripped my hips and drove deeply into me. I cried out, my climax shattering through me as I flew apart. He held me tight, his own rough cry following mine as his release filled me. When I managed to catch my breath, I opened my eyes. He leaned his head back, his rich blue gaze holding mine. We sat there with my cuffed hands linked around his neck. I was plastered against him with him buried inside of me.

"I don't want to move," I said, feeling suddenly vulnerable.

"We don't have to move right now. Maybe in a little bit," he said gruffly.

Relaxing, I leaned back against the steering wheel, accidentally setting off the horn.

"Well, now we might need to move sooner."

"Really?"

"Yeah, we patrol this area actually. It's abandoned. Kids used to get up to all kinds of trouble here."

"I suppose we might be on the way to trouble," I murmured, drawing a finger along his jawline.

"It's fair to say so. I broke all kinds of rules to get your attention. I probably should care, but I don't."

My heart thumped hard as I smiled.

He grinned, giving my hips a squeeze. "Let's get you decent in case anybody shows up. The way it looks right now, I arrested you and fucked you in my car."

"Isn't that what you did?" I asked, laughter bubbling up.

"I suppose so," he finally said with a laugh.

"Was it worth it?" I asked, my laugh fading and vulnerability creeping in again.

His gaze sobered, and he nodded. "Every minute of it."

I carefully untangled myself from him. As I settled into the passenger seat, I glanced up. "You even have mistletoe," I said when I caught sight of it hanging from his rearview mirror.

"That I do."

"I know people are supposed to kiss under the mistletoe, but what's it mean anyway?"

Finn angled his head to the side. "My sister insisted on it. She says it brings love and peace." He paused, his gaze sobering. "I went along with it because for me... You're it."

EPILOGUE

Finn

One year later

It was a year later to the day from when I 'arrested' Jana. I was meeting her at a holiday party held at Daisy and Tristan's place. As soon as Daisy swung the door open, my eyes landed on Jana. She stood in the archway, a glass of wine in her hand. She wiggled her fingers, gesturing for me to come to her. Being besotted as I was, I started walking past Daisy, only stopping when she said my name.

I spun back around. Daisy's eyes crinkled at the corners with her smile. "Were you planning to say hello, Finn?"

"Oh yes. Hello Daisy, how are you?"

"I'm fine. How are you?" she asked sweetly. "It's nice to have you here. It looks like you brought a gift."

I glanced down, realizing I'd forgotten about the gift bag I held in my hand. Jana had ordered the gift for the evening, but I'd been given instructions to pick it up.

"For you," I said, handing the gift bag to Daisy. "No

bloody idea what it is. I was just doing as I was told," I explained.

Daisy laughed and waved me toward Jana. "Carry on," she said with a grin.

I walked over to Jana, immediately dipping my head and dropping a kiss on her neck, pulling her close. I'd been in London for a few weeks and had just returned to Seattle last night. In the past year, I'd finally resigned my position as a police officer. I'd set up a foundation with funding and services for victims of domestic violence and hired an attorney to negotiate strategies to heed the rights of defendants while resolving problems with endless continuances for victims. Ray Sutton had eventually had his day in court. He had been convicted of felony assault against his now ex-wife after far too many continuances.

Lynne Sutton had held up through the long waiting period for the trial, if only because Ray put himself in a worse position by violating the original no contact order. She was involved in the work with my foundation. While I'd resigned from active duty, I stayed on to do training with new officers. With Jana finishing law school, she'd shifted into a different role in the practice with Zoe and was busy being a brilliant defense attorney.

I drew back with a smile when Jana nipped at my ear. When I met her gaze, she tilted her head to the side. "You forgot something."

"What? I took care of picking up the present. I already..."

She shook her head slowly, sliding her hand along my belt. "Your cuffs. You promised..."

"I didn't forget."

She flashed a grin and shrugged, stepping back at the sound of her name.

Zoe walked over to join us, two glasses of wine in her hands. "Want one?" she asked.

At my nod, she handed me the glass of wine. Within

moments, Ethan had joined us, and we meandered into the living room. The evening wore on with Jana nestled at my side on the couch. After we left and I slipped into the car beside her, her eyes caught on the cuffs hanging on the stick shift.

"Aha. This is where you left them," she said with a sly grin.

I no longer had my patrol car for obvious reasons. I returned her grin. "I thought it was fitting."

"What's fitting?"

I hooked my finger over the cool metal and lifted them, the light catching on the ring dangling from one of the cuffs. She grabbed them for me, her eyes slamming to mine.

"Is this...?"

My throat tightened with emotion as I stared into her eyes. "I thought it made the most sense to ask you this way considering how we met. I can't imagine living without you so..."

My words trailed off when a tear rolled down her cheek. Suddenly, she nodded and flung herself at me, promptly bumping her head against the rearview mirror in between us.

"Yes, yes!"

"You didn't let me finish," I murmured with a laugh into her hair.

She drew back, her eyes bright with tears. "I interrupt a lot. That's one of the things I love about you. You don't mind."

As I chuckled softly, my heart pounding steady and true, she held her hand out.

"Where's the key?" she asked, her eyes on the silver band dangling around the cuffs.

With her in a lush pile of curves on my lap, I had to maneuver to get my hand in my pocket, but I managed. I handed the small key to her. Once she had the cuffs open, I slipped the ring on her finger.

Thank you for reading Naughty Wish - I hope you loved
Jana & Finn's story!

For another holiday story, check out All I Want. Dallas was
the sexy fantasy of Audrey's teenage years - her best friend's
older brother and out of reach. An unexpected kiss years
later was never forgotten... until they end up trapped
together on the snowy coast of Maine for Christmas. A
second chance, friends to lover holiday romance that will
leave you breathless - don't miss Dallas' story!

Keep reading for a sneak peek!

Be sure to sign up for my newsletter for the latest news,
teasers & more! Click here to sign up: http://
jhcroixauthor.com/subscribe/

DALLAS

Snowflakes floated down from the night sky, skidding off my windshield as I drove north. I rolled my neck from side to side in a weak attempt to ease the tension bundled there. The digital clock on my dash told me it was past midnight, and I'd not so wisely left Boston when it was already dark for my drive to Maine. Through the darkness, the highway sign loomed. Haven's Bay showed clearly in the darkness, the light snow doing little to obscure the view. The moment I saw the sign, tension unspooled inside me. Haven's Bay was the place I went when I needed to get away, although I hadn't been here in almost four years. It was home in a way that nowhere else was.

A short trip on a side highway and then I was traveling through the quiet downtown. Holiday lights glimmered through the falling snow. The town might as well have been straight out of a postcard with old colonial homes lining its streets, trees decorated with lights and a tall Christmas tree standing in the center of town. No one was around. Hell, who would be at this hour when it was barely above ten degrees outside and snowing?

A winding road led out of town, and I turned off onto another long road. This was past the lovely, manicured part of town where the locals who'd been here for years and years lived. It was a mix of mansions and beach cottages. Lobstermen and fishermen rubbed elbows with the wealthy in Haven's Bay. The common link was their love of the ocean, their family's roots here in Maine, and the hardiness to stand strong through the harsh winters.

I passed by a car half in the ditch. I slowed to check to see if anyone needed help, but whoever had slid off the road was gone. I figured someone else had come along to help.

Despite the cold, I rolled my window down, savoring the salty scent of the ocean rushing through the window. I turned down a familiar driveway. I was about halfway down when my headlights illuminated a figure walking down the drive. My focus had been hazy because I was absorbing the feeling of coming home. Otherwise, I'd have noticed the lone pair of footprints along the side of the drive sooner. Everything sharpened. Aside from desperately needing a break from work, I was here in Haven's Bay for a reason. An old family friend had asked me to check on their home over the holidays. There'd been a rash of burglaries in the area in recent months.

I slowed to a stop beside the person, rolling down the passenger side window.

"Excuse me, you're..."

I meant to tell the person they were trespassing. My words petered out when I saw who it was. My heart lunged, and my mouth fell open.

"Audrey, what the hell are you doing here?"

I swung into action, climbing out quickly and walking around to her. So many questions tumbled through my mind, I didn't know where to start. I took the heavy bag she had clutched in her hands.

"Dallas?"

"Yup. It's me. I'm sure I have more questions than you, but let's get you inside."

She was covered in snow and visibly shivering despite her fluffy down jacket. Worry rolled through me. It made no sense for her to be walking through the snow in the dark, much less for her to be here. I surmised the car in the ditch belonged to her. She didn't resist when I opened the passenger door and all but shoved her inside. Once I was back in the driver's seat, I cranked the heat up, flicked the interior light on, and looked over at her.

She pushed her hood back with a sigh and turned toward me. Her dark brown hair was damp on the ends, and her hazel eyes looked weary in the soft light. My entire body tightened. I hadn't seen her in five years, and she was as beautiful as ever. With her wide eyes, her high cheekbones, her slightly crooked nose that tipped up at the end, and her lush, full mouth, she was an odd combination of regal and endearing. Oh, and sexy as hell.

I knew where she was supposed to be and where everyone believed her to be, and it most certainly wasn't here in Haven's Bay. It was her father who had asked me to come check on their family home. Her family had long since moved away from here year-round, yet they'd kept the home. I'd grown up just down the street. Our families had been friends until my family blew to bits, but that was another story. Right now, I knew Audrey was supposed to be in Italy on a skiing vacation with her fiancé. In fact, her father, Warren Edwards, had mentioned just last night they'd miss her for the holidays.

"Hi Dallas," Audrey said, her words falling softly through the hum of the heaters blowing over us.

She peeled off her gloves and held her hands in front of the heat, her gaze dropping from mine.

"Aren't you supposed to be in Italy?"

She looked back at me. Bitterness and pain flashed in the

depths of her eyes. She swallowed, the sound audible in the small space of the car.

"I'm not."

"Clearly."

I waited. I was very good at waiting. I also didn't mind silence, no matter how tense it was. This helped immensely in my job as an FBI agent. Most of the time, I loved my job. I savored the chance to sit down with criminals in the interview room and outwait them through the heavy silence until we talked in circles to the heart of whatever dark matter they were tangled within. My skill in interviews and in leading investigations had gotten me promoted quickly through the ranks. This past year had worn on me as I'd overseen an ugly web of an investigation related to human trafficking. My specialty was in untangling financial fraud and money laundering cases. Sometimes following the money led to very sad places.

Right now, the small mystery of why Audrey wasn't in Italy swept the cobwebs of those worries out of my mind. I welcomed something else to fill the space.

"I found out he was seeing someone else," she said, her tone level and flat, as if she was consciously wiping it clean of emotion.

Anger scored through me—hard and fast.

"Matthew was seeing someone else?" I asked, my calm, controlled tone belying the fury I felt inside.

I'd fucking hunt him down and make him pay. Later though. Not now. Not with Audrey sitting beside me, pain coming off of her in waves. I sensed it because I knew her. Too well for my own good.

She was almost always level and controlled. Once, only once, had I seen her let go of her precious control. No matter how hard I'd tried to shove that memory away, it was rather insistent. Audrey was forbidden to me, or so I'd convinced myself. I also wanted her more than any woman. *Ever*. I'd pushed her away because I'd felt I must. Her family meant too much to me. Five years ago when she was home for the summer from college, I'd let things go too far. We'd come so close to fucking, it had taken more discipline than I'd known I had to put a stop to it. She'd been glorious when she let go. I vividly remembered the feel of her slick channel pulsing around my fingers. I gave myself a hard mental shake.

She nodded, her gaze fixed out the window. There was nothing to see but the snow falling softly, and the wind occasionally sending it in little swirls in the darkness.

"He's a fucking idiot."

She looked back at me, weariness lining her features, and lifted one shoulder in a graceful shrug. "It doesn't really matter. Can we get to the house?"

There were so many things I wanted to say, but she was clearly exhausted. That much was obvious. I nodded quickly and started driving. When I said the driveway was long, I meant it. It was almost a full mile long. I used those moments until we reached the half-circle at the end to rein in my fury at Matthew. I needed to pummel the guy, and even then I'd still be angry. Yet, that anger wouldn't do much for Audrey, and Matthew was nowhere near here.

That was another thing I was good at—compartmentalizing. Tucking emotions and details away to save for when the time was right.

I rolled to a stop in front of the house. It might've been five years since I'd seen it, but it was just as I'd remembered. A charming cottage with trees clustered to one side and a lawn stretching behind it. I would be able to see the ocean waves crashing against the rocky shoreline in the morning.

"Wait here," I said before hopping out and jogging through the snow on the front walkway.

I kicked my boots on the threshold as I stepped inside. I quickly turned on some lights and the heat. Spinning to head back outside, I found Audrey dragging her bag out of the back of my SUV. I snagged it from her.

"So much for waiting," I said, hoping to annoy her.

She straightened and rolled her eyes. Perfect. I'd rather her be annoyed than see that bitter, sad look in her eyes just now.

I grabbed my bag out of the back, hooking them both in one hand. She walked alongside me, kicking at the snow on the slate walkway with her boots.

In short order, we were inside. She went upstairs to shower, while I took stock of what was available in the kitchen.

I spun around when I heard footsteps. Audrey stood there, her glossy brown hair falling around her shoulders. She wore a faded sweatshirt and cotton pants that clung to her curves.

My cock twitched, and I ignored it. Just because I wanted Audrey and had ever since she'd been old enough for me to think about her that way didn't mean I could have her.

She crossed her arms and eyed me.

"Tell me why you don't want me," she said, her eyes flashing and dark.

Her question was so out of the blue I was unprepared. A bolt of lust hit me so hard, it nearly buckled my knees. Thank fuck I was standing beside the counter.

———

Available now!
All I Want

Go here to sign up for information on new releases: http://jhcroixauthor.com/subscribe/

Please enjoy the following excerpt from Take Me Home, another one of my holiday books!

EXCERPT: TAKE ME HOME

Marley Adams walked up the old ski trail, taking in the view around her. The air held a bite of winter though fall had yet to entirely pass. Cresting the top of the trail where an abandoned ski lift sat, she turned and looked behind her. Her breath caught in her throat. Kachemak Bay lay sparkling in the sun. Mountains rose behind it on the far shore, snow-tipped and bright. She was home. Home was Diamond Creek, Alaska, a fishing village, and tourist mecca in South-central Alaska. Breathtaking views, wildlife galore, and a tight-knit community of independent, quirky souls comprised Diamond Creek. The place she thought she couldn't wait to get away from once she graduated high school. Today, she let her heart soak it in, the one and only place that ever felt like home.

She breathed in the bracing autumn air, scented with spruce and the hint of snow to come. The ground danced with color. Most of fall in Alaska happened underfoot as the landscape was heavily forested with evergreens. She turned around and eyed the ski lift. The lift swayed and creaked in the breeze. It felt like a lifetime ago when her parents had brought her up here with her sister to ski when they were little girls. The exhilaration of rushing down the bunny slope and tumbling into the soft net at the bottom was vivid in her memory. Sometime during her childhood, the ski lodge had closed and stayed empty all the years since. When she was younger, she'd wander through the woods onto the old trails, always wishing it was still open. A place that had been filled with activity all winter long lay quiet and still for many long years.

Curiosity drew her to walk up to the tiny building by the lift. She wiped her arm over the smudged window and peered inside. A woodstove sat in the corner and a bench along one wall. A first aid kit was on the floor and a discarded jacket on the bench.

"Excuse me, are you aware you're trespassing?"

Marley leapt away from the window with a squeak, whirling around to find a man leaning against the corner of the building. The man in question had short brown hair, gray eyes, sharp features, and a body that looked as if it had been sculpted in stone. Even though it was chilly enough for her to wear a lightweight jacket, he wore nothing over the t-shirt that hugged his muscled chest and arms. His legs were rock-hard and encased in sleek running pants. He looked as if he was out for a run. His gray eyes held hers. They were bright gray as if they held lightning inside. His energy was potent masculinity. He didn't seem unfriendly, but neither did he appear welcoming. Against all reason, her body hummed at the sight of him. He was just...pure man.

"You startled me," she finally replied.

The man arched a brow and remained silent.

"Um, I hiked up the old ski trail. I didn't know that was a problem. We used to do it all the time when I was growing up."

The man nodded slowly. His gray eyes left her and traveled around the view, landing back on the small building he leaned against. "Right. Should have guessed that," he finally said, bringing his eyes to hers again.

Marley had never seen this man and though she'd lived away from Diamond Creek for over a decade, she came home for visits every year and knew most of the locals. If she didn't know them, her parents did. As far as she knew, no one had lived at Last Frontier Lodge for years. Residents still lamented its closure.

"Are you from around here?" she finally asked.

The man's mouth tightened. If she'd known him, she might have thought sadness flashed through his eyes.

"Depends on how you define that."

"I grew up in Diamond Creek. I used to ski here when I was a little girl. I haven't lived in town for a while, but last I heard, this place was closed and empty." She took a breath, gathering her courage. Whoever this man was, he had a hell of an effect on her. She couldn't even think clearly enough to introduce herself. "I'm Marley Adams. I live down the road from here." She gestured vaguely in the direction of the little cabin on her parents' property where she'd recently moved.

Those gray eyes landed on her again. For a minute, she thought he wasn't going to respond. He cleared his throat. "I'm Gage Hamilton. My grandparents used to own this place. I was born in Diamond Creek, but my parents moved away when I was little. My, uh..." He paused and closed his eyes, grimacing slightly. When he opened his eyes again, she knew what she saw was sadness. "...grandmother died recently and left the lodge to me and my siblings. I always loved it here when we came to visit, so I moved here. I'm planning to fix the place up and reopen, hopefully this winter."

"Oh. I'm so sorry about your grandmother," Marley said, uncertain what else to offer.

Gage nodded tightly. "Thanks. I was pretty close to her. Still getting used to the fact that she's gone."

Marley nodded, curiosity swirling inside, but she sensed

now wasn't the time to ask the many questions as she had. "It's great you're planning to reopen the ski lodge. People still talk about it back when it was open. Aside from staying busy with locals, this place was hopping all winter long with tourists."

"That's what I'm hoping for." He paused and glanced at her again, his eyes softer. "I didn't mean to sound harsh when I asked about the trespassing thing. I came up for a run and didn't know who you were, so…"

"Oh, it's okay. You should know plenty of locals hike up here and use the old trails for cross-country skiing. It's not like people don't know someone else owns it, it's just no one's been here for so long, people forget."

Gage nodded slowly. "I was thinking maybe I should make some kind of announcement, but I haven't quite sorted out the details yet."

"Oh. Well, as soon as word travels that you're here and plan to reopen, you might want to be ready for lots of people showing up to say hi," she said wryly. "Diamond Creek's a small town. This is big news."

Gage smiled, and Marley thought she might swoon. Dear God, it was dangerous for him to smile. When he wasn't smiling, he had that whole, smoldering sexy and kind of intimidating vibe—just intimidating enough to keep her body in check. When he smiled, her body spun like a top inside—heat and electricity swirling. His eyes crinkled at the corners, the gray brightening and his mouth softening.

Get a grip, Marley. You've known this man for less than five minutes. If she let her body talk, all she could think about was what it would feel like to run her hands over his body, which was nothing short of a miracle.

Gage cleared his throat. "So how far away do you live from here?"

"About a quarter mile down the road from the entrance to the lodge. My parents own about ten acres adjacent to the lodge. Their house is further down the road. I moved into a small cabin they used to rent out to tourists in the summer. It's tiny, but it's got everything I need."

Gage nodded. "Well, feel free to walk around here as much as you want. I suppose I'd better come up with some kind of plan to handle the locals hikers, huh?"

Marley shrugged. "People won't expect to be able to do whatever they want. Once you get this place up and running, you won't need to worry. You might want to notify the town hall and maybe put a notice up in the paper. Otherwise, someone might call the police if they don't know who you are and see you around the property."

Gage threw his head back with a laugh. Her stomach burst full of butterflies. She shook her head and forced herself to look away.

"I'll take it as a good sign that I have to worry about that." Gage followed her gaze out over the bay. "Well, I'm gonna keep running. Sounds like I'll see you around."

She nodded. "I'm sure you will. If you need anything, just stop by. You can see my place from the entrance to the lodge. It's the little cabin with a red roof sitting on the hill nearby."

Gage grinned. "I've seen it. Good to know. Well, I'm off. Enjoy your walk," he said with a quick wave before he took off running. He went around the ski lift and turned up onto the next trail nearby—a much steeper and more advanced trail—and proceeded to run up at a steady pace. Marley had never run up that trail, but she knew without a doubt, it would be grucling. He ran without his pace changing. No wonder he was in such good shape. She finally turned away and began her descent, the view stretching before her.

For the first time in months, she obsessed about something other than the crash and burn of her grand plans to make something of herself. Gage filled her mind—his rock hard body, his sensual mouth...and whoever he was behind his guarded nature.

———

Available now!
<u>Take Me Home</u>

Go here to sign up for information on new releases: http://jhcroixauthor.com/subscribe/

Brit Boys Sports Romance

The Play
Big Win
Out Of Bounds
Play Me
Naughty Wish

Swoon Series

This Crazy Love
Wait For Me
Break My Fall
Truly Madly Mine

Into The Fire Series

Burn For Me
Slow Burn
Burn So Bad
Hot Mess
Burn So Good
Sweet Fire
Play With Fire
Melt With You
Burn For You
Crash & Burn

Diamond Creek Alaska Novels

When Love Comes
Follow Love
Love Unbroken
Love Untamed
Tumble Into Love
Christmas Nights

Last Frontier Lodge Novels

Christmas on the Last Frontier
Love at Last
Just This Once
Falling Fast
Stay With Me
When We Fall

ACKNOWLEDGMENTS

It's fun to write stories when the characters beg you for it. In this case, Jana did just that and so did my readers. Laura Kingsley is never afraid to tell it to me straight when she edits. Yoly Cortez has the patience of a saint and makes magic with every cover. My proofreader angels - Janine, Beth P., Terri D., Terri E., & Heather H. - thank you so much for your kindness!

My husband and family are forever supportive.

My readers - so many thanks in so many ways.

xoxo

J.H. Croix

ABOUT THE AUTHOR

USA Today Bestselling Author J. H. Croix lives in a small town in the historical farmlands of Maine with her husband and two spoiled dogs. Croix writes steamy contemporary romance with sassy women and alpha men who aren't afraid to show some emotion. Her love for quirky small-towns and the characters that inhabit them shines through in her writing. Take a walk on the wild side of romance with her bestselling novels!

Places you can find me:
jhcroixauthor.com
jhcroix@jhcroix.com